THE FOUND WORLD

HUGO NAVIKOV

SEVERED PRESS
HOBART TASMANIA

THE FOUND WORLD

Copyright © 2018 Severed Press

WWW.SEVEREDPRESS.COM

All rights reserved. No part of this book may be reproduced or transmitted in any form or by any electronic or mechanical means, including photocopying, recording or by any information and retrieval system, without the written permission of the publisher and author, except where permitted by law. This novel is a work of fiction. Names, characters, places and incidents are the product of the author's imagination, or are used fictitiously. Any resemblance to actual events, locales or persons, living or dead, is purely coincidental.

ISBN: 978-1-925840-07-0

All rights reserved.

The man sitting alone at the center of the middle bench seat of the Sikorsky S-76 helicopter barely looked out either window at the jungle foliage as they landed a few hundred feet from the clearing made for the carnival. Six heavily muscled commandos in tactical gear sat three across on the bench in front of him and the one behind. Up front sat the pilot and the also-heavily muscled commander of the paramilitary troop. The man's name was not Lathrop, but that is what he went by when on assignment. The mercenaries were under his nominal command, but they were not under his employ. The people he worked for had contracted these "soldiers," much to his dislike. The fact that they were paid by the same entity didn't mean he had to sit next to the beasts, however.

If Lathrop had been given his druthers, it would have been himself and the pilot in a much less ostentatious mode of travel. His tasseled attaché, which matched the tassels on his pair of Bolviant Verrocchios, was his weapon of choice. It was loaded with ammunition—contracts and legal papers that served as modern letters of marque, enough to take down entire governments if his employer wished. But not just ammunition: within the galuchat attaché case were untraceable bearer bonds each worth millions of dollars and pre-signed deeds to properties in Dubai and Tokyo worth even more. It contained carrots as well as sticks.

Lathrop had once been asked by a contracted assassin why he didn't simply take a few for himself and disappear. Lathrop laughed and told him that owning every single piece of property in Hong Kong wouldn't be worth losing his life, which would be lost horribly, once his employer found him again. And—make no mistake, he told the assassin, who was erased from existence once his mission was completed just for asking the question—his employer *would* find him again in short order.

Just like they had found Brett Russell, the man he had come to see. This man used to work for Lathrop's own employer before he uncovered a shocking truth, but then went underground, promising to exact retribution one day. This didn't bother the Organization; one man, or an army of them, or even a nation full of oath-sworn revengers couldn't do any real damage to those pulling the world's strings.

What *did* bother them was losing a man of Brett Russell's talents. He once liberated an entire mining village while simultaneously fighting what the Organization believed was an actual living *Spinosaurus* in the depths of the Congo rainforest. He was the perfect candidate to help them secure an asset so valuable that made the entire contents of Lathrop's galuchet case look like bag of glass marbles. The Organization would have him hand over the attaché in a second if Brett Russell would accept it for the job.

But they knew he wouldn't. All the wealth in the world meant nothing to a man wanting only revenge. So, the man not really named Lathrop would offer him revenge.

He allowed the commandos to exit one side and come around to slide open the door on the other side for the others to get out. He stood on the soft dirt, the heels of his astronomically expensive buffalo-hide shoes sinking half an inch or so. They would need to be discarded after this adventure, he thought, but others would be waiting for him when he stopped in New York on his way back to Geneva. It would amuse him to have his man drop the old pair of $2,000 shows into a box at the Goodwill. Maybe he'd see a hobo wearing them next time he was in the city and chuckle to himself that the bum could have bought himself a car to live in.

A small beetle almost immediately alit upon the right lapel of his bespoke Ermenegildo Zegna suit, which made Lathrop very nearly smile; the bug had good taste. He swept it off and looked at the spectacle drawing cheers and excited gasps from the loose crowd of farmers and their lead-poisoned children. He believed he was near the "city" of Ipixuna in Brazil, a settlement of about 17,000 and one of the most difficult to reach anywhere in the Amazon rainforest, which was saying something.

To the Organization, however, nothing was terribly difficult to reach. To get Lathrop and the troops to the spot outside Ipixuna, the 12-seat S-76 was dropped out of an enormous Antonov An-225 Mriya cargo plane, having first been loaded onto an automated Chase XCG-20 glider, which descended to and leveled off at 5,000 feet, at which time it was slowed to stalling speed. At that moment, a radio signal was sent to set off the bay door's explosive bolts, which blew off the hatch and allowed the Sikorsky to slide out, its rotors already in motion. The glider crashed somewhere nearby and the helicopter flew the thirty miles or so to the target location, this godforsaken bit of swampland where the idiot carnival was set up to entrance the dullards hired to destroy their own habitat. The Organization had no hand in that, but Lathrop thought it sounded like something they would do if it suited them.

Some 200 feet ahead was a dome made from chain-link fencing, the onlookers gathering around its perimeter. The two dozen spectators turned and glanced briefly at the sight of a massive helicopter unloading black-clad soldiers carrying assault weapons and a polished white man wearing intentionally incongruous city clothing, but then turned back. Whatever was inside the 200-foot diameter of that fenced dome must have been compelling, indeed. Lathrop knew what was inside the dome: Brett Russell. God knew what he was doing, but it was enough to make sustenance farmers walk away from their crops in the middle of a spring day perfect for planting.

The dome itself had been erected in such a way that some jungle trees were almost entirely within it, full of weird rainforest creatures that Lathrop, frankly, could do without ever encountering. He spent his days in Geneva, one of the most civilized places in the entire world. His friend the beetle had been a novelty; one just didn't encounter insects where he conducted Organization business. That said, a poisonous monkey or spitting lizard would be more than a novelty and would constitute something entirely unwelcome on or near his person. He might have to ask one of the commandos to remove it for destruction, and he preferred not to ask anything of the thugs if it could be avoided.

When Lathrop finally made it to the fence, the farmers parting more in suspicion than awe at his appearance at the dome, he saw what they were all gaping at: inside was the man whom he knew to be Brett Russell. There weren't going to be a lot of Caucasians this deep into the jungle, making it easier to identify the man he was looking for—this was fortunate for Lathrop, because the man inside the caged area was almost unrecognizable as the man in the photograph he had been given by the Organization. The Russell in the picture had been a man in the field locating and, when necessary, fighting cryptids that usually turned out to be "only" giant bears, undiscovered killer condor-like birds, and that *dinosaur* in Congo: lots of muscle and hard as hell. But what Brett Russell was now made the old Russell look like an agoraphobic accountant. Lathrop had never met the actor they called "The Rock," but he imagined Russell looked like what The Rock was 5' 11" instead of his ridiculous 6' 5" and had earned his muscles by fighting man-eating monsters instead of lifting free weights with personal trainers.

Russell's muscles, as impressive as they looked, weren't for show—they couldn't be. This was because inside the dome, standing in the waist-deep brown water of the inlet dug to drain from the main river a hundred feet, the man was wrestling with—Lathrop literally had to blink a few times to make sure he was seeing what he thought he was seeing—a black caiman crocodile. It wasn't the 16-foot monster that full-grown adults were, but the adolescent was at least 10 feet long, bigger than most man-eaters in the world already. It was *huge* and Russell could barely keep his gigantic arm around its neck as it thrashed and tried to take him apart.

Lathrop's mouth actually dropped open, and he looked at the farmers on either side of him for confirmation that he was seeing what he was seeing. But they didn't look away from Russell being thrown around as the caiman tried to fling him off and escape through a submerged gate in the fence that led back to the river. (There was a man, probably the fight organizer, squatting just outside the fence with his hand on a handle for the gate; he must have been the one who would let the monster back into the river once the fight was over, one way or another. This told Lathrop that Russell didn't intend to kill the animal, which agreed with the dossier he had read on his target.)

The black caiman may have been trying instead to fling him off and then kill him, which it could do easily if it could get Russell got in front of his giant maw. Alligators and crocodiles, Lathrop knew, worked to tire out their prey by spinning and thrashing; if Russell got too tired to hold on, it would be the end of him.

It seemed impossible that this wasn't the first time the man had fought for a few Brazilian reals … but it also seemed highly unlikely it *was* the first time, since it looked like he was the one who was getting his enemy too tired to fight and not the other way around.

As Lathrop looked closer, he could see that Russell had anchored himself onto the caiman's back with a strap, so it wasn't quite as impossible as it looked. It still looked completely impossible to him, but maybe not so ridiculous as to be entirely unbelievable. Russell had his arm under the strap and this helped him get his flesh raked open by the spines on the giant animal's hide. He also had black sleeves, really long black gloves, almost all the way up his arms that, Lathrop was sure, kept him from being sliced open by the rough skin of his enemy.

The equipment, however, seemed to be there just to make it possible for Russell to last long enough to get tired and be ripped to shreds by the croc. The fact that even with all the thrashing, the caiman hadn't been able to get Russell into a position where he could bite him in half was testament to the power of the mountain of muscle the man had become. And not just muscle, of course—the way Russell moved with the animal showed that he knew what he was doing.

This was definitely not the first time he had done this, which was almost literally unbelievable. Lathrop's superiors hadn't been exaggerating. Before him was perhaps the only man for the job they wanted to hire him for.

The squatting fight organizer craned his neck, looking at something in the water trench leading from the river to the gate. He smiled in surprise, then very obviously looked at Russell fighting the caiman, then looked back at the trench ... and lifted the handle to open the gate.

The assembled onlookers let out a collective *oooh* when they saw what had happened. Lathrop couldn't see what was going on, but then, he didn't know what to look for like the locals. Soon enough, though, it was unmistakable: a thick snake, a *giant* snake, swam into the enclosure, where Russell and the enormous crocodile didn't notice it since they were fighting possibly to the death.

He fumbled out his secure smartphone, thumbed open the translation app, and said into it, "What is that thing?" He held it out to the sweaty brown man next to him, to whom it spoke in weirdly British-accented Portuguese, "*O que é essa coisa?*"

The wide-eyed man laughed and said at the phone like he was speaking to a person inside it: "*Anaconda verde.*"

Lathrop didn't need the phone to translate that: it was a green anaconda. The green anaconda was the largest snake in the world. And it was now swimming in a wide circle around Brett Russell and the enormous crocodile. It could kill a human pretty easily—and since anacondas were constrictors, once it wrapped around a man, he couldn't get out no matter how strong he was. Lathrop noticed a large dagger on Russell's belt—why the hell hadn't he used it on the killer crocodile?—but if the snake wrapped around his torso, there would be no way for him to get it out, let alone do anything with it.

Finally, one of the farmers pointed and shouted to Russell, "*Serpente!*"

In the middle of trying to heave the caiman toward the gate, which the little promoter fellow still had open, Russell stopped and looked to where the farmer was pointing. He didn't have to search—the 15-foot-long anaconda was hard to miss, especially as its new circle was smaller than the first as it moved closer to Russell and the crocodile. Then he whipped his gaze at the promoter with steely anger, a look that almost made the little man fall over with fright.

As if he'd heard Lathrop think of the dagger, Russell pulled it from its sheath. The crocodile took advantage of the distraction, however, and snapped at his hand, making Russell drop it into the opaque water. He took only a moment to recover from this, however, and threw himself around the caiman's neck. In a series of heaves across the water, Russell got the huge animal to the gate, which was all the croc needed to get the hell out of there.

Lathrop marveled. *Could he have done that at any time? Was he just making a show for the paying customers?*

The look in his eyes at the approaching anaconda, however, betrayed real alarm—maybe even fear—and he moved to duck under the gate and get himself out of there as well. But when he ducked, the promoter let the fence fall the whole six feet to the bottom of the trench leading into the enclosure.

In surprise and real anger, Russell yelled at him: *"Deixe-me sair, seu bastardo!"*

Lathrop needed no translation to understand that. But the promoter gestured toward the crowd, which was now in a frenzy of betting with a man that had to be the man's gambling agent. He must have been willing to part with his star attraction for whatever money the ecstatic wagers would be bringing in, because no human, not even one looking like The Rock's big brother, could survive an encounter with a trapped and possibly panicked green anaconda.

And here it came. If Brett could get to the other side of the water, which was at least fifty feet away, he could get onto the ground and be safe for at least a few minutes from the snake, long enough to tear his way through the cheap fence if he had to. But the anaconda was between him and the other side and would be upon him long before he could wade or swim the distance.

It approached. In ten more feet, it could start winding around him, and death would be swift after that. Lathrop knew that it was a myth that constrictors cut off the air of their victims and so those attacked had three or four minutes to be rescued; in fact, boas and anacondas squeezed their prey so hard that it cut off the blood to the heart. Without immediate CPR—highly unlikely inside a cage surrounded by illiterate farmers in a tiny village in the Amazon rainforest—the stopped heart would stay stopped, and Brett Russell would die before Lathrop got the opportunity to make the Organization's offer.

He motioned to the commander and said, "Shoot the snake."

The commander didn't laugh or ask why. Instead, he immediately called over one of his troops—his second-in-command, probably—and said, "Mister Lathrop wants that snake killed."

The second-in-command laughed and asked, "Why?"

"Since when do you ask *why*, soldier?" the commander barked.

Lathrop shook his head. The time it took for that exchange made it impossible to get a clean shot at the snake before it would go behind Russell and begin coiling around him. *Brilliant*, he thought. *All the guns in the world and not a brain cell among them.* He didn't look forward to reporting this immediate failure to his superiors.

Russell, however, seemed to know that no help was coming, not from the promoter, the spectators, or the man in the suit and his idiot brigade. His eyes darted around, taking in the snake coming nearer, the wet ground around the makeshift pond, the snake, the fencing, the snake, and the trees above. Maybe he would try to … no, Lathrop had no idea what Russell was thinking about doing. Russell was a dead man, and maybe Lathrop would be as well when he returned. The Organization had done more for less.

Then a look of recognition appeared on Russell's face, and even though he strained to see what the man could have spotted in the tree branches fifteen feet above him, he could see nothing but bark and shiny leaves.

The snake curled around Russell now, and there was nothing in the world that he could do to stop it. He must have known it, too, because he ignored the anaconda even as it finished the first coil and moved around for the second, not squeezing yet, just getting into position.

But Russell put both hands under the water and swept his belt out through its loops, keeping his hands above the level at which the snake was about to tighten around him. He closed one eye and aimed and whipped the belt up at a specific point on the lowest tree branch. The buckle struck something, which fell as a yellow blur and splashed in the water not two feet away from him. Right before the anaconda finished its final coil and was about to crush the arteries of Russell's heart, he threw himself forward to grab the object with his glove-covered hand. Squeezing his eyes shut and turning his head with his mouth tightly closed, he crushed the thing against the snake's skin. Lathrop could see that Russell was crushing it because a strange ooze burst from under his palm, seeping out against the green scales of the monster.

What the hell is going on? Lathrop literally had no idea what he was watching as the anaconda not only didn't finish the job and fatally tighten around Russell's body, but it shook, jerked, and finally slackened unto death, floating now without moving at the surface of the water. Russell held up his hand so the crowd—and the promoter, who looked very much like he had just emptied his bowels into his pants—could see. Lathrop didn't understand what the yellow-crusted pancake of unidentifiable biomass represented.

Words spoken in admiration, even awe, rippled through the crowd: "*Sapo veneno.*" Every single man present muttered it, even the ashen-faced promoter.

Lathrop was about to say the words into his phone when mercenary commander Crane said, "That's a goddamn poison dart frog."

"What?"

"That guy just knocked that poison dart frog out of that tree and smooshed it against that goddamn killer snake."

Lathrop goggled. "He just killed a fifteen-foot green anaconda ... with a *frog?*"

"Sir, that right there is—well, *was*—a Golden Poison Frog. It's what, two inches long? That little sucker has enough poison in it to kill *twenty* full-size men. That damn snake never had a chance. That dude would also be dead without whatever those gloves are. I'm thinking Kevlar, like the gloves shark hunters wear. I want some of those now."

It's like daycare with Uzis, Lathrop thought, but said only, "When he gets out of there, bring him to me. Try not to talk too much. You're not good at it."

Crane nodded, not sentient enough to know he'd just been insulted, and marched over to where Russell was just emerging from the cage, having swum to the bottom, lifted the gate fencing enough to get through, and emerged like the Predator from the steaming brown water to stand in front of the visibly shaking promoter.

He looked back at Lathrop. "Maybe I should give him a minute."

Lathrop nodded. The man wasn't as dumb as he looked. (He couldn't be.) But letting this play out before interrupting Russell did seem like a prudent idea.

Russell grabbed the promoter by the neck, his fingers reaching almost all the way across. This inspired a renewed frenzy of wagering among the still-engrossed farmers, and the promoter's second seemed all too happy to cash in on this latest development and probable advancement opportunity.

The scene was taking place only about 150 feet from where Lathrop had been watching, and he could see plainly as Russell lifted the glove that was covered with the Golden Poison Frog's entrails for the promoter's careful consideration. Russell said, "*Eu deveria fazer você comer isso,*" which made the farmers laugh and made the promoter soil himself anew.

He didn't bother to ask anyone what that meant. You didn't hold up a hand full of incredibly deadly poison while holding a man by the neck in order to tell him the weather. Russell let go of the man's neck, but it was extremely clear that he was not to move an inch.

Using the other gloved hand to very carefully remove the first glove, Russell then used the gloved hand and his booted foot to slowly turn the stiff first glove inside-out. Then he lifted it and shoved it against the promoter's chest, saying, "*Lave isso.*" The farmers cracked up again, saying "*Ooooh!*" like they were in grade school.

Lathrop didn't know Portuguese, but he did know enough Spanish to figure out, along with the men's derisive laughter, that Russell had essentially just told the pants-crapping man: *Clean that*. It was more threatening than it sounded, because merely touching the skin of the Golden Poison Frog for an instant would mean paralysis. Anything more would bring a quick but very painful death. He put out his hand, palm up. *Pay me*.

The promoter pulled a wad of damp bills from his pocket and laid it in Russell's gloveless hand. Russell looked at it, gave the promoter a smile, then punched him in the gut so hard that nobody watching felt like they'd be able to stand up straight for a week. The little bitch remained on the moist ground, unable or possibly unwilling to move. Russell spit on the promoter to make sure he was still alive, and when the man moaned, he said, "*Novo cinturão, também.*"

Lathrop turned with a quizzical look at the farmer standing next to him, who laughed. He must have known English, because he saw the look on Lathrop's face and said with a smile in his heavy accent, "He want a new belt, too."

~~~

The bulk of humanity trudged toward Lathrop and the paramilitary troops, passing them by without a single word or glance. Whatever had happened to Brett Russell in the two years since the Organization sent him to Congo, it had made him into … Lathrop didn't know what. But it was scary as hell to him, and he thought he had seen everything there was to be scared of in the world. Still, he had a job to do: "Brett Russell?"

The man stopped immediately, then turned his muscled back and neck to fix Lathrop with a gaze so hateful that it made him want to run back to the helicopter, job be damned. "*What*," was all Russell said, not turning the rest of the way but just standing there with the rest of his body in position to resume walking away.

"I'm Mister Lathrop with—"

"I know who you're with. You're with a troop of goons and wearing a $20,000 suit. You're from the Organization." The sneer in his voice was unmistakable. "What do you want? If they wanted to kill me, they would've already carpet-bombed this entire town. So what is it?"

"Don't you want to know how we found you?"

"It's the *Organization*." He raised his eyebrows. "So, I'm going to start walking again in three seconds. One. Two—"

"I'm on the run myself," Lathrop said rapidly. "I want to talk to you about your revenge."

Russell narrowed his eyes at the man, sizing up his claim. Finally, he shrugged and said, "Mister Fancy can buy me *uma cerveja*. The goons wait outside."

~~~

Once they were ensconced in a corner of the steamy bar, Brett refusing to sit with his back to the door, Lathrop started in: "Let me show you something, Mister Russell. Actually, may I call you Brett?"

"Go ahead. Then I'll rip your eyeballs out and drop them in your beer."

"Mister Russell," Lathrop said with a shaky smile, "I have a stack of stolen bearer bonds worth a total of eighty million American dollars in my satchel. I would offer them to you—"

"Save your breath," Brett said, and moved to get up.

"—*but* I know that isn't what interests you."

He sat back. "You stole them? From the Organization? How are you still alive?"

"You saw my troops out there." At Brett's supremely unimpressed expression, he continued, "Which wouldn't scare the big bosses, I know. But maybe it's enough to keep freelance assassins from cashing in. But really, the Organization doesn't realize yet that I've gone rogue."

"I see."

"You don't see. You think I'm lying, but you're sticking around for a moment to amuse yourself with *why*."

Brett shrugged. "Maybe. Why don't you tell me *why*, then? Why have you gone rogue from people who can have you killed like they're brushing a beetle off their suit?" Lathrop visibly started at that, which made Brett smile. "For money? You have to know that you wouldn't have two weeks to enjoy that money or what it could buy for you. Besides, I see that suit and those shoes. You had, or maybe still have, access to that kind of money, anyway. So not money. Why'd you go rogue? If you *did* go rogue, which I got to tell you, I really don't believe."

"Your family was murdered to keep you loyal, correct?"

Now it was Brett's turn to recoil in surprise. He nodded warily.

"The same was done to me. First they threatened it, and then they did it. Which still makes no sense to me, as I was as loyal as they come. Perhaps it was a power trip; I don't know, and what's more, I don't care. I want to exact revenge on them the same as you do."

"Open your wallet."

"What?"

Brett leaned forward and took a fistful of Lathrop's $200 shirt and $100 silk necktie, clamping them so firmly that they would have to be thrown away, since they would never come uncreased. "If they took your family from you ..." he said, and reached into his own shirt, pulling out military-style dog tags engraved with the faces of his wife and daughter. "... then you keep them close to you every second of every day."

Lathrop very slowly reached into the breast pocket of his suit jacket and pulled out his billfold. Inside were pictures of himself with a woman and young boy, then photos of what must have been his wife and child together and individually. "Yes," was all Lathrop said.

Brett let go of the man's clothes and sat back in his chair. He said after a few seconds of thought, "Those could be fakes you carried on you just to convince me."

"Of course they could," Lathrop said. "Just as yours could be fake as well. But they're not, and neither are mine. Now, may we speak about what I traveled all the way here to speak to you about?"

"Maybe. But first, if you're on the outs with the Organization, how did you find me? They must have told you where I was, and it wasn't because they wanted to help you get revenge against them by contacting another target of their sick loyalty plan. And you couldn't have found me on your own. I don't even understand how they could, except that *that's what they do*." At Lathrop's nod, he went on: "So? Why did they share my location with you? However they figured out or were told my location, they gave that information to you. Whether you are, or were, their employee or some kind of contracted intermediary, instead of sending just Thug Life out there to shoot me down? You got the information from them; more than that—they *gave* it to you. Amuse me: tell me *why*."

"You're quite right, of course," Lathrop said, then took a sip of his beer now that things seemed to have relaxed slightly. "I did work for them, the same as you used to, working in a front corporation until they needed more for a particular assignment. In this case, they wanted me to find you because of your experienced hunting and killing cryptids of all kinds, including at least one actual dinosaur, that *Spinosaurus* in Africa."

"I never killed anything unless it was about to kill me, and even then I tried not to. I laid Bras out back there because he forced me to kill that beautiful green anaconda to save my own life. And the *Spinosaurus*, by the way, is still alive with its young in the Congolese rainforest. But all right, they wanted someone with my skills."

"Yes. They want you to go somewhere that man has never been, so deep into the jungle that it has never been mapped, in order to bring back an Organization scientist and the ... well, the *superweapon* he created."

Brett's eyes narrowed again. "Wait. There's a scientist there, but no man has ever been to this place in the jungle."

"Right, sorry—before him, I mean."

"Uh huh. And I assume he was being paid by the Organization to develop this 'superweapon'? What is it, a nuclear bomb?"

"No," Lathrop said with a chuckle, "they have access to nuclear bombs if they want them. But using nuclear weapons would be bad for the global economy, to say the least, and the Organization *is* the global economy, in many ways."

"All right, so what is it?"

Lathrop cleared his throat awkwardly. "There I have to demur, Mister Russell. I don't actually know. I believe they didn't consider me to have a 'need to know.' They just needed me to know enough to hire you to find this scientist and, if possible, his superweapon, and bring your quarry back to the opening of the secret world."

"Secret world," Brett repeated.

"Don't concern yourself with that at the moment, if you please. What I'm trying to tell you is that they want that man and his weapon desperately, enough to hire you instead of killing you so that you may retrieve them for the Organization. When I realized how mad they were to get this done, I saw it as my opportunity to exact revenge upon them for what they did to me, to my wife and son."

Brett nodded slowly. "All right, then. Your revenge would be, what, selling their superweapon or whatever to the highest bidder that wasn't also somehow them?"

"That is my business, Mister Russell. Maybe I want to drop it on their heads. That's no concern of yours. Your concern is only what I ask of you and what I am willing to pay you."

"You say you know money doesn't interest me, although I will take those bonds in addition to whatever your real payment is, give the money to the people of Ipixuna so they don't have to slash and burn their own rainforest to survive. But what are you *really* trying to pay me with?"

Lathrop cleared his throat again, but this time it was anything but awkwardly. He sat straighter in his chair and arranged his suit just so, then said, "When I left Geneva for New York to get your dossier and the bonds with which to bribe you—the Organization is unable to see that money cannot buy anything worth possessing—I was already planning to betray them. With the information and the bonds, I was able to steal documents showing exactly who it was who ordered the execution of your family. It is with those documents that I shall pay you for retrieving the scientist and his creation."

Brett leaped across the table, breaking it as he dove into Lathrop and they crashed through Lathrop's chair onto the floor. He bared his teeth like a mad animal and snarled into the Organization man's face, "*WHO IS IT? Tell me right now or I'll crush your skull.*"

Weirdly, other than the natural alarm from being attacked and driven to the dirty floor, Lathrop remained calm. "I never looked at the papers, *Brett*. Do you think I wasn't aware that you would torture me until I told you what I knew? Now *get off of me* before I whistle for my dogs to shoot you dead."

After a moment, Brett relented and helped Lathrop to his feet. He unfolded some of the reals and gave them to the barkeep for the damage, then sat at the next table over with Lathrop. "Where are these documents?"

"They will be waiting for you when you emerge from the secret world. If I am lying and I don't have them, then I imagine you would kill me right then and there, or later if I somehow were able to get away. But, as you can see, I'm not concerned, because I really do have them in a very safe place. As a goodwill gesture, however, I'll give you the $80 million in bearer bonds right now." He pushed the inordinately expensive attaché across the table, and Brett took it and placed it next to him on the floor. Lathrop laughed and said, "Aren't you going to check them?"

"Doesn't matter," Brett said. "What's this 'secret world'? How do I find this scientist? Give me the details, and we just might have a deal."

Lathrop ordered them another round, and within half an hour, he had told Brett Russell absolutely everything he knew about what he called the secret world, the rogue scientist, and how enraged the Organization would be when they didn't get what they wanted. He finished with, "They might kill you, but they will definitely kill me. But that won't matter; then I'll just be with my family."

For a minute, Brett just stared at Lathrop and considered everything he'd been told and been offered. Then he nodded and said, "All right. But I'm gonna need my team."

~~~

In the eleven months since she had left her husband in the rainforests of South American, television journalist Ellie White (formerly Ellie White-Russell) had worked every spare moment to get her life and career back to where it was before she had met Brett Russell while covering the story of an alleged Kasai Rex in the jungles of Congo for the program *Cryptids Alive!* But everywhere she turned, everything she tried, her efforts to get in front of the camera and start reporting once again were thwarted as if by some mysterious hand.

She knew what this "hand" was: it was the Organization, that shadowy global cabal that was after Brett. She had hidden out with him in the rainforests of South America for a year, married him in some 400-person village called Pijuayal, but finally she could take living half a life no longer and had to leave. In the end, Brett had seemed relieved; looking over his shoulder for both of them was exacting a terrible toll on him, and he would be better able to survive in peace without her.

Men—always men—approached her almost weekly for months thereafter in Iquito, where she had been stranded, unable to command the fare for passage home. They offered her money or threatened her life, sometimes both, in pursuit of information about where he was now. Early on, she told them about Pijuayal, since she was certain he would have left there probably within days of her departure. They paid her well for the information, some $4,000, which allowed her to get back to the United States and begin her life again.

Or so she had thought. The bastards must have thought she was holding out on them even when she was back in Atlanta: she noticed suit-wearing men tailing her on city streets, watching her from across the street when she was home, even going through her mail and her garbage, she was sure. If they didn't have her phone tapped, she would have been very surprised.

But it was all for nothing, because she hadn't spoken to or heard one word from Brett in over a year. The Organization must have been trying to squeeze her, because every job opportunity mysteriously closed even after they had agreed to hire her. She wasn't yet thirty and was still, if she could say so herself, extremely hot in a Kim Possible action *grrl* kind of way. Anybody should have wanted her talking into a microphone on their TVs or computers.

But then came *The Mysterious Investigators*. The offer to be the face of the paranormal investigation show came out of nowhere, just when she was about to apply for a job at a Starbucks in Fort Wayne, Indianapolis, which was where she was going to have to move and live with her sister. She thought doing this would make death not seem like much of a change when it finally happened, hopefully sooner than later.

Not that *TMI* was a huge step up financially, but at least it allowed her to do what she loved, which was paranormal documentary filmmaking. The two guys running the show, Stefan and Ravi, wanted a female investigator to help expand their YouTube subscriber demographic, as well as come up with some new ideas. The weird thing was that *they* found *her*. She had her LinkedIn profile and her own (non-remunerative) YouTube channel, so it wasn't all that weird, but still, it worked out.

Now, a couple of months in, she and Stefan were working on the "Biloxi Leprechaun" episode at the industrial park studio *TMI* rented when Ravi came in with an opened letter in his hand and a dazed look on his face. Stefan, who was as tall and Nordic as Ravi was petite and Indian (although both were second-generation Americans), sat back from the editing monitor and looked at their partner. "Oh, God. What?"

Ellie was sure the letter was some kind of eviction notice for the studio or maybe a crackpot death threat from something claiming *TMI* was "too close to the truth" on some garbage conspiracy idea or another. But Ravi smiled dreamily, and she knew this was something else entirely.

"We got a grant," Ravi said, his white teeth gleaming. "I don't even remember applying for it, but *The Mysterious Investigators* just got a grant from …" He read from the page: "from the Skeptic Skeptic Society."

"The what?" Ellie asked with a laugh.

He read further, "The Skeptic Skeptic Society is dedicated to exposing skeptics of paranormal phenomena as 'the real phonies.'"

"That sounds legit," Stefan said with complete sarcasm.

"Right? But they're funding us to go down to the South Atlantic—like *way* south—to shoot an episode on the …" he trailed off, the look on his face falling from dreamy to disappointed.

Ellie and Stefan waited again, then prompted Ravi with, "Come on! On the *what?*"

"On, um, the secret civilization living under Queen Mary's Peak, the cone of the main island's volcano." Ravi looked longingly at another piece of paper that had been folded into the main letter. "God, I wish this wasn't a bunch of bullshit."

Ellie didn't feel disappointed, because crackpots and nutters were part and parcel of investigating occult and paranormal topics. For every living dinosaur, there were twenty "secret Nazi installations" or, frankly, "Biloxi leprechauns." She said, "Why is this getting you down, Rav?"

Ravi looked away from the letter and showed them the front of the enclosed item. "They included a check for us to get started before they would bring us out there. It's for $100,000." He turned it back around and gazed at it wistfully again. "It looks so real, though."

Ellie stood and nipped the paper out of his hand and looked at it. "It really does," she said, surprised, since she expected it to be handwritten on some paranormal crank's personal account. But not only was it on thick paper with the name and address of *The Skeptic Skeptic Society* … it was a cashier's check.

Now Stefan slipped it from her fingers and looked at it himself. "This was done on real cashier's check equipment. It may be fake and worthless, but it would look exactly like this if it was real."

"It's not real," Ellie said.

He met the eyes of his compatriots and said, "One way to find out. I'm going down to the bank."

Ellie and Ravi didn't ask to come with. They just got their coats.

~~~

The check was real.

"Get the equipment," Ellie said before they had even left the bank. "The letter says we need to be in Cape Town in two days to get the ship to the island."

"They don't have an airport?" Stefan said, more as a statement of unwelcome fact than as a question.

"Guess not. I hope we can get a flight to South Africa on such short notice."

Ravi laughed and interjected, "With $100,000, I bet we can convince an airline to find it in their hearts to get us some seats." He pulled out his phone as they walked out into the Atlanta humidity, and thumbed around for a minute. "Yep, KLM can get us there leaving tomorrow. Which is good if we want to get there in time for the boat, 'cause it's a twenty-hour flight."

Ellie and Stefan groaned, but this was the opportunity of a lifetime for all of them personally as well as for *The Mysterious Investigators*. "I'm gonna need like fifteen phone chargers," Stefan said, "but I guess I can afford it now."

~~~

Orville "Popcorn" Blum called on a student at the very back of the class, a tall troublemaker wearing one of the snapback hip-hop baseball caps even though school rules specifically banned such headwear inside the building. But Popcorn knew better than to challenge a student in front of his friends in an inner-city high school. Or anywhere else. Two other teachers had been forced to move to other schools after getting their faces pounded in by aggrieved "students," and Popcorn was intent on not joining their ranks. "Yes, Marvin? I mean, 'DJ Passport,' did you have something to add regarding the slope of an angle?"

"It's 'DJ *Pump-Pump*,' man, and hell, no, I don't. I been meanin' to ask forever—why you look like Fat Albert with glasses? A young brother wearin' a red sweater and talkin' 'bout X and Y? You an embarrassment."

Popcorn—a nickname he enjoyed but never told another *teacher* at this "prison prep" school in deepest, darkest Detroit, let alone a student—was used to this by now. He was sick of it, but after he dumped a $2 million windfall into developing his own hyper-parallel quantum-based neural-net computer system and lost it all, Teach for America was the only job he could get that didn't involve steaming milk for lattes. "That is an excellent question … which I'm not going to dignify with—"

The heavily scarred wooden door with a metal grill across what used to be a window swung open and a man and a woman, both dressed like Secret Service agents, stepped into the room. The woman asked crisply, "Orville Blum?"

The class exploded with riotous laughter. Literally riotous—they threw their already-tattered textbooks into the air, fell onto the cracked tile floor screaming with mirth, and knocked over desks in their spasmodic throes of disbelief at their teacher's given name. Popcorn paid them no attention and answered the visitors, "I am he."

If the students had been laughing before, now they were screaming and gasping for air.

"We represent an interest that would like to hire you to sail to an isolated island and run the technology for a historic scientific mission."

He had felt excitement at the beginning of that sentence but was crestfallen by its end. He had once had a *very* bad experience on a research ship and vowed never to do it again, and he told this to the duo.

"We will pay you one hundred thousand dollars," the man said, "in advance."

That froze every student in place; money talked even when these kids would listen to nothing else. Popcorn looked at them and their surprised paralysis and, without another word, walked out of the classroom with the two agents. Before he went through the door, however, he called to 'DJ Pump-Pump' and said something so foul, so insulting, that Teach for America would have fired him on the spot no matter how desperate they were for bodies at the front of classrooms.

Marvin jumped to his feet and made to rush his teacher, but the female agent had her Glock out before he could take two steps. He immediately stopped cold. Once Popcorn was safely out of the room, the agent holstered her weapon and threw a gang sign at the humiliated student, one she knew would be effective judging by the colors of his clothing.

Popcorn saw this and realized he would have *paid* a hundred grand to witness it, and he had gotten it for free. Whatever this adventure was, boat or no boat, he was in.

~~~

The *Slangkop II* was a cargo and passenger ship registered out of South Africa that usually made the voyage from Cape Town to Tristan da Cunha only in spring each year, but Lathrop had been able to convince the vessel's owners to make an extra trip. It would take five days by ship, which was an insane amount of time where the Organization was concerned, but the weapon couldn't be yanked up by any helicopter that would fit inside the cargo hold of an airplane like when he and the troops were dropped into the Amazon to get Brett Russell. Besides, he had other assets, just not ones that were as likely to succeed as Russell and his party.

Lathrop had gotten the people Russell had asked for: Ellie White, her two fellow dipstick video documentarians, and the tech whiz-kid Popcorn Blum. Also on the ship, in addition to the twenty or so crew members and Captain Bantu, was Lathrop himself, Commander Crane, and Crane's half a dozen commandos. Since the *Slangkop II* was built to carry one hundred Antarctic research station workers all around the

South Atlantic in forty-six cabins, carrying just thirteen people in an addition to the crew made for a strangely quiet experience.

"It's got a gym," Commander Crane said to Lathrop as they stood on the deck, watching the steel gray water meet the steel gray sky. The entire vista was utterly featureless in every direction. They would be to the island in about six hours, but any sign of Queen Mary's Peak had yet to appear.

"It has a library, too, not that you'd be interested in that," Lathrop said. "I don't know, maybe it has comic books you'd like."

Crane faux-punched him in the arm like he was being ribbed by an old pal. *You're not even a moron*, Lathrop thought, but decided there was no reason to antagonize the muscle-laden man, who could probably kill him with a single real punch. "So we got a team in there already?"

We? Lathrop shook off the man's presumption and answered, "As my superiors briefed me—and *you*, as you were in the room with your eyes open, at the very least—they were able to re-breach the opening that Merco discovered and had sealed to hide the weapon and himself."

"Merco?"

Lathrop shut his eyes. "Doctor Merco," he said. "The *scientist* we're trying to recover?"

"Oh, right, I thought you meant somebody else." Crane took a large bite out of one of the creatine energy bars he always seemed to have on his person. "They got in, but nobody's heard from them since, huh?"

"That's what they tell me, Commander. Thus, we are staging this incursion as if the earlier one had never taken place. Hence the redundant armory we carry with us. And hence the need for a ship with 10-ton winches. And hence why you and your men are here." Lathrop didn't really know why he was bothering to explain to Crane what the man already had been told—it would be lost again, most likely—but Brett Russell was certainly not speaking to someone he (correctly) suspected of still working for the Organization, and it had been almost five full days of dreary isolation. If an albatross had been following the ship, and not one bird or fish had been seen for two days, Lathrop probably would have been talking to that.

"Wait, you said *re*-breached? Like they had to reopen the mountain to get in again?"

Lathrop would have been more impressed, but Crane was, for all his apelike stupidity, an excellent paramilitary mercenary, and "breached" would be a word contained within his vocabulary of military verbs. "Yes, indeed. Apparently, Merco and whoever he was working with made sure to somehow close up the entry within the volcanic cone. *How* he did it is a complete mystery, although how where he gained entry was plainly visible to the team there before us as a large scar on the side of the mountain."

Crane's eyes narrowed a little, almost as if he were having a thought of some kind. "But, Mister Lathrop, aren't volcanoes filled with lava? How can you open one up and get—"

"Don't," Lathrop said, and pinched the bridge of his nose between two fingers. "Just ... *don't*. Suffice to say that the Tristan da Cunha volcano hasn't blown since 1961. Besides, Organization scientists believe he went into the side of the volcano and down, perhaps under it. We lost radio contact with the first team as soon as they opened the scar and went in, which would happen if they were underground."

"And never got out."

Lathrop nodded. "A month would be a long time to be lounging on the beach on the Organization's dime if they *had* gotten out, so yes, one must assume they're still down there, dead or alive."

"So ... *we* could be killed, too."

Is this guy serious? "Well, *yes*, Crane. If it weren't dangerous, we wouldn't need an extraction team with assault weapons and rocket-propelled grenades." He watched it sink in to the mercenary, and it was more clear than ever why he and his impressive-looking band of soldiers of fortune had been drummed out of Special Ops: a soldier who didn't know he could die was a soldier who endangered everyone around him. "And please refrain from the use of 'we' in this context; I shall be waiting upon the *Slangkop* for your return with the traitorous Doctor Merco. Probably in the library."

Crane nodded, then after a moment let out a laugh the cause of which Lathrop was completely unable to discern. Crane said with another faux-punch in the arm, "You like comic books, too!"

~~~

It wasn't until chow on the second day that Brett Russell ran into his ex-wife. He saw her first, or rather, he recognized her first, since the only way she looked different was that her chestnut hair was longer and, impossibly, she looked even more beautiful. Ellie looked almost straight at him but obviously didn't realize who he was, probably because of the deep mahogany tan and huge muscles he had acquired after an additional year in the jungles of the Amazon. Lathrop intuited all of this merely by watching the two of them for a few moments, then filed it away in case he needed to use it for leverage of some kind later.

It was only when Lathrop cleared his throat to get the mess hall's attention and introduced each member of their exploration party that Ellie sat suddenly straight at the table she shared with a tall blond and a short Indian and stared at Brett with her mouth agape. He laughed and gave her a little wave from across the compartment. When Lathrop finished his introductions, he started right into the briefing, but the wide smiles Ellie and Brett shared with each other didn't stop the whole time.

"Lady and gentlemen, you are all being paid very handsomely to be here. Mister Russell is receiving something more valuable than mere financial reward for his role, but the rest of you are each to be paid one of the bearer bonds secreted in a vault back in Cape Town for your assistance in this affair: ten million dollars each."

Despite the fact that every man present knew of his (and her) reward, many of them still whistled at the size of their payday. Lathrop would have smiled, but it wasn't particularly amusing; he encountered people almost every day of his career who received similarly enormous payments for their cooperation with the Organization. And the Organization did pay—the fact that many recipients couldn't handle that much wealth at once and ended up dead within two years required no effort by Lathrop's employer. The $130 million that would be paid for this caper would be made back through the auction of Merco's weapon within one month.

"With this much on the line, I trust you will each listen to the following with the care it deserves, as I have told none of you other than Commander Crane and his compatriots what you are to do for this money."

He motioned for a slim woman Brett hadn't seen all day on the ship—he hadn't seen anyone, really, except for Popcorn, who hadn't known Ellie at all but was excited to meet her—to come forward with a 55-inch television hooked up to a sleek laptop computer. She handed Lathrop a small remote control and stepped back into the shadows of the galley. In a moment, everyone there had forgotten she was there.

Lathrop turned on the television and, after a few clicks, a computer-generated map of the island appeared on the screen. "In whatever role assigned to you by Brett Russell, who is the leader of the civilian end of this expedition and requested you specifically, you will enter a subterranean area of unknown size in order to locate and retrieve—by force, if necessary—the former Organization scientist Doctor Gaffney Merco. His weapon, the size of which is also unknown, will be extracted with the good doctor and brought back to the ship, whereupon it will return to the mainland for transport back to Geneva, Switzerland. Is anyone here unaware of 'the Organization'?"

The scowls Lathrop took in told him that everyone was familiar.

"I am a rogue agent of this world cabal, and getting Doctor Merco into my hands will be a great blow against the Organization."

"Wait," came a lummox voice from the table where the commandos were seated. It was Crane. "You're not with them anymore? I thought you said—"

"For God's sake, shut up, Commander." He smoothed his tie and regained his composure. "You'll have to forgive Commander Crane, who is the leader of the paramilitary end of the operation. He has the body of a god but the brain of a developmentally disabled insect."

"There's a gym here," Crane said to the room.

"In any case, one does not advertise that he is 'on the outs' with the Organization, as several people on this very vessel can attest," Lathrop said. "Believe me or don't, it makes no difference to your role in this mission. I will be paying the bearer bonds and whatever other remuneration I previously arranged with Mister Russell, regardless."

The burning look in Russell's eyes made Lathrop very nearly gulp with anxiety, because of course he was lying. If he told the man the truth, Russell might have just killed him in the Amazon on general principles even if it would cost him the opportunity to get the names of those who had ordered the hit on his wife and son, as well as those hired killers who carried out the murders. For this operation, however, that "might" was decisive; Lathrop was forced to risk having his neck broken by Brett Russell or not carry out the instructions of his superiors in the Organization. The latter was *much* more frightening to consider.

That in mind, Lathrop continued, "We will make landfall tonight. At first light tomorrow, you will proceed to the eponymous mountain of this volcanic island, Tristan da Cunha. There should be an opening in the cone where Doctor Merco and whatever gang of pacifists accompanied him entered the mountain."

That took everyone in the compartment a moment, even the commandos who already knew about it. "Whoa, whoa, *whoa*," Russell said, his voice louder with each repetition, "they went inside a volcano. *From the side?* That doesn't make any sense. Yeah, volcanoes are basically hollow, but they're not like an upside-down ice cream cone."

"Of course that's true with every volcano on Earth ... except this one. Somehow—no one in the Organization knew how, or at least they didn't tell me they knew—Merco discovered an entire subterranean world under the island, and he considered it the ideal place to live out the rest of his days so the weapon couldn't be found and he couldn't be forced to share the plans for the weapon with those who had paid for it."

Lathrop realized he was sounding more sympathetic to the Organization than one who was trying to damage it would be, but he wasn't terribly concerned about that at this point. What were they going to do, let Brett Russell keep them from their millions? He highly doubted that.

He went on: "Merco entered through the volcano as I have explained, but not before sending a long encoded message to his daughter back in Austria that described what he'd found and what he was doing, both with himself and with the superweapon he had developed and built using Organization funds. That's how we know where he went."

"We?" Popcorn Blum said. "Do you mean 'they'?"

Dammit. "Yes, of course. Old habits die hard."

"*You're* going to die hard if I find out you're still with those sons of bitches," Russell growled.

"Right, thank you for the *machismo*, Mister Russell." He clicked the remote and the view from above to one looking at the island from sea level. He clicked again and a deep chamber appeared without detail underneath the island on the screen. It was far bigger than the island, its length on the screen looking about twice that of the island above it. "The island covers about 80 square miles, so an area of twice the length with the same width would be about three hundred square miles."

Ravi whistled, impressed.

"Exactly. It's a lot of ground to cover. But that's why we have the world's foremost cryptid hunter leading the team."

A puzzled-looking Ellie White rose her hand and said, "I understand the jungle expertise, but there must be a thousand seasoned rainforest explorers. But you wanted Brett and my team—did this Doctor Merco report cryptid activity under the island?"

"Please say yes," Stefan said in excitement, making the rest of the room chuckle. This would be something to put *The Mysterious Investigators* into the history *and* science books forever.

Lathrop didn't chuckle or even smile. He simply said, "Yes, he did. We don't know what, but his daughter shared all of his messages with us, and he told her there were all sorts of … unusual creatures."

Russell didn't raise his hand to talk. "Why do I get the feeling that Merco's daughter didn't give you this information out of the kindness of her heart. Or for all the bearer bonds in the world. She's dead, isn't she? Died shortly after your goons came for a visit, I bet."

Everyone in the compartment looked at Russell and then at Lathrop, and their gazes remained on the well-dressed Organization man. There was no point in denying it—these people were either in or out, and "out" was pretty much impossible unless they wanted to swim back to Cape Town. So Lathrop told them, "You are correct, Mister Russell, but she died by her own hand, not by the efforts of any Organization interrogator—" He stopped dead and closed his eyes. *Dammit, dammit, DAMMIT.*

"Holy crap, you *tortured* her, didn't you?" Russell spat and got to his feet. "You tortured her for the messages and then she killed herself because she'd never be able to get over what you did to her. And making her sell out her own father to his death." The big man took two angry steps toward Lathrop but stopped when the muzzle of an AK-47 was pressed against the side of his head. He slowly turned to look at Commander Crane, who shook his head.

"Sit down, Mister Brett Russell," Crane said. Russell went back and sat down, choosing to die—or kill—another day.

"Now," Lathrop continued sharply to the shocked faces around the compartment, "there are believed to be many unknown animals and other lifeforms in this subterranean world. That's why all the heavy military equipment has accompanied us on this little adventure. We will land at the only inhabited area. From there, we will head to the entry point. Now, let's discuss the extraction itself. Doctor Merco is—"

WHOMMPRRRRRRRRRR

The entire ship bucked and the metal of the hull groaned with the stress of being forced sideways like it had been broadsided full-speed by an oil tanker. Everyone threw themselves around chairs or tables bolted to the floor as everything else slid at a 45-degree angle against the bulkhead with the hurling of the ship to port.

~~~

Brett hit the deck and held fast to the secured base of the table. As the whole ship rocked, Ellie came sliding by, picking up speed as she approached the very solid-looking bulkhead. But Brett stuck out his big arm and looped it around his ex-wife before she could slide any farther. He looped her back in and held her next to him as others either splayed out on the deck holding on to their own chairs' and tables' bolted-down bases or gripped the chairs and tables themselves. Others just kept sliding until they smacked hard into the metal walls on the lee side of the ship.

The *Slangkop II* stopped listing and began loudly creaking as it swung back the other way. At least this meant the ship wouldn't capsize—but it did mean that everyone who had slid against one bulkhead now started sliding the other way. Some were able to catch the tables and chairs as the angle spent an instant abeam before lolling to the other side.

"Fancy meeting you here!" Brett yelled with a laugh even though they were all certainly about to drown.

"The pleasure is mine!" Ellie yelled back with her own laugh. "Why am I not surprised this is happening when you're involved?"

"You can't blame me for this—I don't even know what's ... happening ..." His eyes went wide as he saw what *was* to blame for what was happening to the ship. *Not even possible.*

Ellie saw his look and turned around still held in his arm out the long series of windows on the side of the ship now lifting from the water. And she screamed.

Then everyone else looked and, to a person, screamed or yelled—it would have been hard to tell the difference. Lathrop, the commandos, definitely Popcorn, everybody cursing and some of them pretty sure they had fallen asleep during the briefing and were having a nightmare.

The gray abomination, its face slick with water still rushing from the prominence of its jaws, was the face of a Chinese dragon and the body of a massive prehistoric eel. It was *huge*, much longer than the ship and probably as wide. And within its jaws were untold rows of impossibly giant and sharp teeth. It had rammed the ship with its enormous head and reared up like a hundred-foot-tall cobra, ready to strike again.

"*Lathrop!*" Brett bellowed across the mess hall, and the Organization man turned, his face seized with dread. "What the hell is going on? *What is this?*"

Lathrop just shook his head. But Brett knew that had to be bull. The ship lolled all the way to starboard, not quite as far as it had to port—so they *wouldn't* be capsizing, thanks God—and when the deck was almost flat again, he wrapped Ellie's arms around the base of the table, then sprinted to where Lathrop held onto a chair and slid until he had grabbed onto it as well.

"You know what this is, goddammit. This is why you brought me. *What is this place?*"

"All right, *all right!* I don't know what in the name of Heaven that *thing* is out there, but I told you we thought there might be unknown animals—"

"*Unknown animals?!?* That's a frickin' Chinese dragon on super-steroids!"

"No kidding, Mister Russell, I hadn't noticed," Lathrop said, able to be ironic even in the present situation. "We had no idea what animals there might be. That's what 'unknown' means, you ape."

Brett was about to reply with something really witty, but suddenly the dragon's hideous grin filled the view out the port side and it smashed against the ship, making every window explode and spray those inside with hailstones of safety glass. The side of the ship buckled and one of the commandos who had slid against that bulkhead was launched into the air, his body already broken, and flew right through the glass of one of the starboard windows, shattering it and falling into the sea below.

"*Abandon ship!*" called a voice heavy with an African accent as the *Slangkop II* rolled onto its starboard side. It was Captain Bantu, who must have rushed down from the bridge despite the danger. "When she lifts from the water again, get to the lifeboats on the starboard side!"

"Which side is that?" Crane yelled, his confusion at the term seeming much stronger than his fear at being attacked by a sea monster.

"*The right side, idiot!*" Lathrop shouted, making Brett think the Organization really needed to put its people through some sensitivity training for communicating with the workforce of today.

But right and left were confused at the moment because the ship didn't stop rolling. Impossibly cold water rushed through the open windows as the starboard side was submerged and they headed for going completely upside-down, *Poseidon Adventure* style. Everyone who had been able to hold onto the bolted-down furniture of the mess hall hung on for dear life at what was now the ceiling. Those who hadn't been able to grab hold of anything—the male Organization agent and two of Bantu's crewmen—were swept out of the ship as the water rushed out again during its continued roll to surface on its port side. They ended up lolling nauseatingly, but at least they didn't remain capsized, upside-down in the water.

"Brett!" Ellie yelled to him, "We have to get off the ship!"

"Go get in a lifeboat—I'll catch up! *Go!*"

The outsize head of the dragon serpent crashed to the surface of the water as the beast tried a different attack. It plunged underwater, which to Brett looked more dangerous than it just ramming the ship. An enemy unseen was an enemy with an advantage.

But that was secondary for the moment. Brett stood with Lathrop's shirt once again bunched in his fist. "If the underground world is where the cryptids live, then *what is this?* Why is this thing out in the open water? *Tell me!*"

Lathrop hesitated but then obviously saw no advantage to be had in prevarication and said, "Merco must have left the opening to the subterranean ecosystem open. Part of that opening must incorporate a lagoon or other water access, and that *thing* must have swum out of that opening. I'm as shocked as you are; one might expect this on land there, but—"

"Whoa—a giant sea serpent is something we should have *expected?* What in God's name is down there?"

"I mean in general," Lathrop said, completely sidestepping the question, then turned his gaze to someone standing twenty feet behind Brett, apparently waiting for a break in the "conversation" to address his boss. "Crane, some assistance would be appreciated. What in blazes am I paying you for?"

"Not bodyguard service, I'm pretty sure," Crane said. "I just wanna ask: what do you want us to do with the weapons. Leave 'em on the boat, or take 'em with us? We can't take the heavy stuff in the lifeboats. Like *heavy*. The lifeboat wouldn't float."

Lathrop asked in a near-whisper to Brett, "Could you please unhand me? I'm not going to be staying on the ship, obviously, and these dolts need guidance if we're to have any chance at all of finding Merco. You may 'rough me up' at a more convenient time for all of us."

Brett sneered and shoved Lathrop away. "Don't assume the boat is necessarily—"

The three men plus the soldiers were hurled into the overhead as the serpent came from under the boat and rammed in from beneath, into the hull a few decks directly below the mess hall. One of the commandos, who was at the immediate epicenter of impact, shrieked in pain, his ankles and knees shattered. The five other mercenaries, plus Crane, Blake, and Lathrop, seemed not too much worse for wear, but they were all stunned by hitting the overhead and then smashing back down onto the deck, groaning and trying to remain conscious.

"Get the weapons into the lifeboats and get out of here!" Lathrop yelled to Crane, who for once seemed to understand something told to him and ordered the four uninjured men out of the compartment. He followed them and began barking orders amidst the shouts and occasional scream coming from those in the lifeboats already on the water.

"You're not leaving yet," Brett said to Lathrop as he watched Captain Bantu run toward the bridge, no doubt to assess the damage to the *Slangkop*. "There's something you need that's still on this boat. But you can't have your goons get it. Why not? What is it?"

"You're talking nonsense, Mister Russell."

"Then let's go. Follow me—I'll rescue your sorry ass." He moved to exit the mess hall but stopped when he noticed Lathrop wasn't behind him. "What? Tell me what the thing is, and maybe I'll help you get it."

Lathrop opened his mouth to respond, but a rending and buckling of metal roared through the ship as the middle of the vessel collapsed, sending rushing sea water up to their ankles in a matter of seconds.

Still, even though his pallor showed the terror within him, Lathrop used the fixed tables and chairs to help steady and propel him toward the staircase to the area with his cabin.

"You're not going down with the ship, you son of a bitch!" Brett yelled at him and, casting a regretful eye at the lifeboats he could see out the window, launched himself to follow the Organization man and grab him and drag him out if need be. There was no way the fool was going to a watery grave still possessing the secrets he had promised to Brett. The others could access their bearer bonds, but Lathrop hadn't told Brett where his information was, so Brett would have to keep the weasel alive until he had it. Not much point to surviving himself if he lost this chance to enact his revenge.

Before Lathrop made it to the hatch to the cabins, Captain Bantu appeared in front of him. "The ship is going down. Get to a lifeboat while you still can!"

"Out of my way, sir!" Lathrop ordered, but the water was to everyone's mid-shin now and it was time to live or die. "I *need* something from my cabin!"

"You *need* to be on a lifeboat or you will go down with the ship. Once everyone is off, only then may *I* not go down with the ship! Get off of my boat—the longer a boat is near the ship, the more chance it will be eaten by that sea monster! You all must get away *now!*"

As if on cue, screams arose from the lifeboats as the dragon serpent slid through the water, opened its enormous jaws, and consumed a lifeboat filled with *Slangkop II* crew members. Then it went under again to swallow and digest its meal. Even a giant cryptid sea creature had to obey the laws of biology, and eating something the size of a lifeboat would take at least a few minutes to be ready for another. There were still leagues to go before they could reach the island, and it would take perhaps an entire day to row to it. But for any of them to stand a chance, their mariner Captain Bantu was the only one who could navigate them there on the open sea. Bantu had to survive.

Ellie had to survive.

Brett, not so much, even though he would prefer being alive to hurt those who hurt him. His survival was optional, and the sea serpent's survival could not be allowed if anyone was to make it to dry land. They could call for help on the satphones (if they had them on the lifeboats), but no help could get here in time to save every boat from being eaten whole by the monster.

That gave Brett a brilliant, or possibly brilliantly stupid, idea. He said to Lathrop, who was up to his waist in freezing water now but still trying to push through Bantu to get whatever the hell was so important in his cabin, "The equipment in the hold—are there explosives in there?"

"Of course there are. We might need to blast a new tunnel if they sealed it off behind them ... although it seems like it might already be open."

"Ya think?" Brett snapped, but focused again: "Which container?"

"I don't know *that*." Lathrop looked annoyed at him; he must have been highly committed to being annoyed if he could shine through with that while they were all about to die. "Perhaps the solid captain here can—"

Bantu named the container ID immediately. He looked at Lathrop's surprise and said, "I know everything that happens on my ship."

"Is there a code to arm them?"

Lathrop goggled at him. "Are you serious? They're underwater already! You can't get to them, you moron!"

Brett didn't hesitate: he punched Lathrop in the middle of the chest, just far enough off the sternum not to break it with his knuckles. Lathrop buckled and puked into the swirling water. "Sorry, I didn't hear you. *Is there a code to arm them?*" He raised a fist in a plain threat to smash his fist into some point on Lathrop's body once again.

"Fine! It's written in indelible marker when you open the control hatch!" At Brett's look, he said, "Crane forgets things."

Brett lowered his fist, although he didn't want to—what possible reason could there have been not to tell him anything he wanted to know about arming the explosives? The man was just a complete dick, even though being like that was making it more difficult for Brett to save the man's life. No matter now—he had what he needed. What to do now, he didn't really know yet, but it definitely included reaching and arming those explosives. He said to the captain, "Please drag his sorry carcass to a lifeboat and get out of here. If you possibly can, drop an empty lifeboat but keep it lashed to the ship. I'm hoping our little friend outside will get tempted by it before any of the ones with people actually still in them."

"I cannot leave while you are still on board," Bantu said.

"I appreciate your honor, sir, but you'll kill every one of us if you stop me from doing this. And you staying on board *will* stop me from doing this."

"Doing what?"

"*Get the hell out of here!*" Brett shouted in the captain's face, and he swept by Bantu and Lathrop in the chest-high water to get below decks before it really was too late to save anyone at all.

He rushed down the passageway to the steps he guessed would lead to the cargo hold. He didn't know the layout of the ship, but he did know such vessels in general, and the cargo hold hatch was usually in about the spot where this set of steps led. The water was almost to his neck now, and he would have to dive if he was going to get down there and do what he needed to do.

He took a moment. How long would it take the serpent to be ready for another lifeboat morsel? Brett had no idea, but he didn't have much choice about the timing of getting down there, no matter how long he set the delay on the charges for. When he was in Special Ops, he and his brothers were trained how to hold their breath for a *long* time, and he had been called upon to use that training in the Amazon on more than one occasion over the previous two years. But that had been for only five minutes at the most; his record was eleven minutes. He might need to tie or even break his record for this little stunt.

He took in a huge breath, using his chest and stomach muscles to "store" air by swallowing it, then took another deep breath to fill his lungs and plunged under the rising water.

~~~

The lights stayed on long enough for Brett to get a good look at exactly where the hatch was before he submerged, which he was glad he could do because he'd have to open his eyes in the salt-water environment soon enough, and that was going to *burn*. He could open his eyes for just an instant and then would have to shut them if he was to avoid swelling them up so badly he wouldn't be able to see clearly for hours. And if this sea monster was any indication of what they would be finding under the island, he was going to need his sight to be as good as it could possibly be.

When he had pulled himself along the railing halfway down the metal stairway and was thinking about how glad he was the lights had stayed on this long, he realized with a groan that he had no flashlight or other device in order to see inside the pitch-black cargo hold. He knew basically where in the compartment the container holding the explosive ordnance was, but he didn't know what kind of mechanisms it used or where the control panel hatch was so he could arm the whole thing to blow. He couldn't hold his breath forever—he'd have no time to feel his way around as he tried to locate the damn things in the huge hold. There wasn't likely to be much in the cargo hold except for provisions and the mission's soon-to-be-lost-forever large equipment, so at least he wouldn't have to guess where to start, but still, he knew his chances were slim. His chances and therefore everybody else's chances.

Even if he could hold his breath for an epically long time even for him, once the last of the air-containing ship went under and all of that remaining buoyancy was lost, the iron ship would sink so fast he'd never be able to get out and reach the surface. The fact that he was willing to die didn't mean he wanted to die. Not yet, anyway.

He made it after about twenty seconds to the hatch. He got to the wheel and immediately started turning it, happy that Bantu kept his ship in such good working order that the wheel offered almost no resistance at—

WHOOSHHHH

—the wheel was yanked from his hand as the water in the stairwell burst through the suddenly wide-open hatch. Brett was hurled forward in the wave rushing into the cargo hold, making his eyes pop open and his breath involuntarily escape. He was in dry air for the moment, but that moment wouldn't last long—the ocean was going to fill the giant space in less than two minutes.

However, in the less than two *seconds* that the lights illuminating the cargo space remained on before all electric power was lost and he was able to have his eyes open not underwater, Brett could identify the metal containers marked DANGER: HIGH EXPLOSIVES.

Then it went dark, and although the current carried him toward his target as he swam, by the time he got there the hold was filled. The air-filled compartment might have been the only remaining source of buoyancy keeping the sink from heading right for the bottom, so now the surface might be unreachable within sixty seconds.

Before he went under again, Brett was able to once again swallow air and get some deep into his lungs for his extended breath-holding technique. Now, he was flying blind and the clock was running in several different ways at once. He groped to where he made contact with the container and moved quickly along its twenty-foot length, feeling for anywhere there might be the groove of a panel cover.

There! His fingers reached it and pried it open. He opened his eyes for a second but got nothing but stinging sensation; the only thing visible in the blackness was a tiny white LED display that he wouldn't be able to make out without goggles on, no matter how close he got. The light-emitting diodes did show him that there was a numeric keypad below it, but anything written on the panel door for the idiot commando's reference was completely invisible in the dark.

His air wasn't quite used up yet, but soon it would be and he'd either succumb to a lack of renewed oxygen or he'd inadvertently gasp for air and drown right there. He swooshed his head from side to side, eyes open for an instant and then again, looking for anything that might serve as a light source: another hatch, a goddamn floating flashlight placed there by Poseidon, anything. But there was no light, and so there was no way he could see the code to arm the explosives. Also, there was a new and horrendous creaking of metal, which sounded to Brett very much like a large boat giving up the ghost and being compressed one last time as it slipped beneath the waves for the final time. *No air and no light*, Brett thought, his mind preparing itself for the inevitable. *It's like being deal already—*

KROOOOOONNNNNNNNNNNNNNNG! With an almost unbearably loud shriek of iron tearing, an enormous crack tore through the hull of the cargo hold. Light poured in, even if it was the blue light of the sun as seen from beneath the surface of the ocean. The hold was already full of water, so nothing rushed in and he wasn't swept out. He could see the black writing of the indelible marker now:

CODE: Ø Ø Ø Ø

Crane couldn't remember THAT? Even underwater and about to die, Brett smiled and shook his head. But the smile faded when he heard the continued creak of the hull and then heard a primal screech that he knew could only be from a creature as massive and terrifying as the island's colossal dragon serpent. He also noticed that it didn't feel like the ship was sinking anymore, no increase in water pressure and no floating inertially as the hulk went down.

Then he saw the thing's face again and knew: *It's holding the ship in its jaws.*

Was the sea monster trying to eat the entire *Slangkop II*? He thought that maybe the ship had been torn in two when the rip in the hull of the cargo area occurred, and the beast might have sensed a little morsel was inside this piece. Brett didn't know and he didn't care—he had light and for the next seventy to ninety seconds, he still had oxygen.

He pounded four zeros into the keypad, and a couple of words appeared on the LED display. He squinted as hard as he could, eyes sizzling, but he could only guess it was asking him how long until the charge should explode. He hit what felt like the 3 and the 0 and then what he hoped was ENTER. Maybe he had guessed correctly: the display changed and it looked very much like it could be counting down.

Either way, his time was up—with another deafening rending of metal, the opening in the hull tore open, and Brett could see that another section of the ship had fallen away. The leviathan was gripping this last section, the one Brett and the explosives were in, and bringing it up toward the surface. The sea monster seemed to understand smashing things, and Brett felt sure the thing was about to rear up out of the water and come crashing back down with what was left of the *Slangkop*, destroying everything still in one piece, including Brett.

The cargo hold was yanked out of the water, and Brett was swept out of the ruined hull as the water flowed down out of every breach in the hull. The armed container of high explosives also slid to the opening but was only just too big to fall through. *Air!* As he fell the twenty feet from the ship back into the water, Brett was able to inhale a body-full of sweet oxygen, holding it as he fell back into the water and beneath. On the way down, he opened his salt-painful eyes and saw at least six lifeboats a good distance away, far enough maybe that—*oh, hell!* Brett curled himself into as protective a ball as he could underwater.

The Chinese dragon sea monster crunched down on the ruins of the ship and lifted it higher to bring it down against the concrete-hard surface of the water. As it reached the crest of its swing—*BOOOOOOOOOOM*—the ordnance went off, blasting the serpent's huge head into fifty chunks and separating every part of the ship into automobile-sized blades of burning metal.

The water shook with the force of the explosion. A few seconds later, Brett could feel huge plates of metal slice through the water all around him … but none cut him in half. For a moment, he remained under the water, his held breath keeping him floating toward the surface after his plunge. In a few moments, he bobbed up into the open air. The sea was suffused with the creature's blood, as red as a matador's *muleta*. Sharks would be there soon, monsters devouring monsters. And everything else they could get their teeth into, including Brett.

He took stock of his surroundings. On one side, he could see the lifeboats pretty far off, and beyond that, what could only be the tip of the volcano on Tristan da Cunha. The whole little fleet, including the serpent, must have drifted during the whole nightmare in the direction they had already been heading. Captain Bantu knew what he was doing when he went up to the bridge at the onset of the attack, probably setting the engines to full speed ahead in the direction they needed to go if they were ever to get to the island.

He turned to look in the other direction and saw, on the other end of a thick rope than had been ripped clean through, a lifeboat that had to have been placed in the water but kept with the ship. Although Brett had been thinking bait for the monster, obviously *he* had ended up being the bait. The creature's violent treatment of the *Slangkop II* while Brett was swimming around inside the cargo hold must have severed the rope and sent the lifeboat placidly floating away.

Brett got to the lifeboat, threw himself inside it, took a minute to catch his breath and make sure everything was still connected to his body, and then stuck the oars in the oarlocks and got rowing to catch up with the rest of the survivors. Whoever that might be.

~~~

Brett could hardly believe it, but almost everyone had survived. And Captain Bantu was quite the mariner: he was able to get the shell-shocked occupants of the *Slangkop II*'s lifeboats corralled into a little fleet and land them on the north shore of Tristan da Cunha. Once the boats had been dragged onshore, some of them sinking into the wet sand a bit from the weight of automatic weapons, RPGs, and other armament Crane and his men had been able to grab before the ship went down for the last time. Brett had seen a lot of other, much heavier weaponry in the shipping container housing the explosives, including vehicle-mount machine guns and surface-to-surface missiles. The latter was clear evidence that, whether Lathrop was on the run from the Organization (doubtful) or still fully on their side (which didn't matter, as long as Brett got his information), the global cabal was funding this little adventure and supplying it with arms no other NGO could get it hands on. There also were Jeeps and an entire armored vehicle to mount those guns on; but all was beneath the waves now.

Lathrop, Ellie and her crew, Popcorn, Commander Crane and his four remaining soldiers, Captain Bantu and of his two crewmen were all there and intact. There was also the Organization woman, who didn't seem terribly fazed by what had just befallen them. Surprised, sure, but not fazed. Brett couldn't begin to guess what the woman's story could be.

"Mister Lathrop, we are on land now. I relinquish command to you," said Captain Bantu formally. "We are near the only souls on this island, about one kilometer to our west. There are three hundred people in a village, Edinburgh of the Seven Seas. I will remain there and alert my people about our misfortune. In perhaps a month, there could be another ship here to take us back to Cape Town."

"A *month?*" Popcorn said in horror. "I don't even have my laptop anymore!" Others in the group seemed equally put out, although probably for less whiny reasons.

Lathrop put up a hand. "Not to worry. Once we have secured our prize, there will be transport for our return. There is no airfield here, but Organization helicopters can travel long distances. Now that there will be no heavy equipment coming back, thanks to our sea monster, everything and everyone should be transportable by these conveyances."

"*Organization* helicopters, huh?" Brett said with a cynical tone.

"Believe me or don't believe me, Mister Russell. At this point, I truly could not care less. All that should matter to you is that your payment will be genuine information. As I say, I haven't looked at the dossier and thus cannot be tortured into revealing the contents—"

"I don't torture people," Brett said. "That's what *you* do."

Lathrop must have been very tired by their collective near-death experience, because he actually laughed and waved Brett off like he was an annoying child. "Do stop wasting your breath and everyone's time, Mister Russell. If I possessed in my mind but refused to give you what you seek, you would break every single bone in my body, one by one, until I told it to you. Is that not so?"

Brett chewed his lip for a moment. Finally, he said, "All right. So we can get back in Organization choppers, and you can carry your superweapon in them too, I'm assuming." He looked to the west, where he could see the slimmest sign of human habitation: Edinburgh of the Seven Seas. "Let's get this show on the road."

~~~

The road, when they found it, led to horror.

Edinburgh of the Seven Seas—Bantu told them on the walk over that locals always referred to it either as "the Settlement" or "the Village"—was made up of a few dozen red-roofed buildings that housed the three hundred residents, schooled the children, and comprised the entirety of the economic and social activity on Tristan da Cunha. There were hotels for the visitors and seafarers who stopped on the island for rest or refueling. The few trucks and cars that had made it to the island usually dotted the streets.

But now, just on the main drag that the *Slangkop II* survivors could see when they came around the corner, bodies lay everywhere. Blood literally flowed on the street from dismembered corpses into the storm drains. Bodies and pieces of bodies were scattered as if torn apart by huge animals in mid-run. Nothing moved except botflies buzzing between carcasses on a feeding frenzy.

"D-Do you guys see what I'm seeing?" Stefan asked everyone and no one, the camera he had rescued from the ship hoisted onto his shoulder and capturing the carnage on video.

"I want to leave," Ravi said from right next to him. "I want to leave right now."

"Then you're seeing it."

Brett shut his eyes and said a quick prayer, but like Stefan, it was to anything listening and to no one except himself. He opened them and looked at Lathrop, whose cool demeanor was definitely a little offline as his wide eyes took in the scene. "More escaped cryptids?"

"I ... would assume so. The idiots must have left the portal open."

Brett saw Crane's eyes flicker at *idiots*. They weren't talking about Doctor Merco and his people. "You already sent a team in," he said, forcing himself to turn away from the horrible scene and look squarely at the Organization man. The way he said it, it wasn't a question. "They're the ones who left this 'portal' open. Merco is a scientist—he wouldn't be so sloppy. *And* he probably knew you would send people after him."

Lathrop met his gaze defiantly and said, "Mister Russell, it can come as no surprise to you that seeking your assistance is the very definition of a last resort."

"I thought you brought me in to beat the Organization."

"There are a lot of people *dead* here, you Indiana Jones wannabe, so let's just drop the pretense, shall we? Of *course* I still work for your former employer. They are the ones who tasked me to use *whatever means necessary* to bring back this man who ran off with Organization property—a weapon for which he was paid outrageously, even by Organization standards. All right? I have what I promised you—*any means necessary*, remember? Now, shall we all remain here as tasty morsels while you and I talk about the niceties of my position within the company?"

Brett had no choice but to give in. No boats or helicopters except those contacted and paid for by Lathrop and the Organization would be stopping as Tristan da Cunha for at least a month and possibly much longer. If Lathrop and his apes left Brett and the rest of them there to die, then they would die. So Brett shrugged with feigned insouciance and said, "Fine. But don't be expecting me to save your life if one of these things come after you."

Lathrop smirked and let out a single chuckle. "Mister Russell, until I give you the information I promised, I am literally the safest person on this entire expedition."

At the look on his pale weasel face, Brett punched Lathrop right in the mouth. The well-dressed man stumbled back but didn't fall down; the blow had been the weakest Brett could manage that would still leave an impression. Then Brett turned, patted Ellie on the shoulder to comfort the crying woman for a moment, then started on. "Let's go," he said, and everyone else followed, Lathrop wiping blood from his lip at the back of the line.

~~~

Mangled human bodies along with several corpses of large and heroic-looking dogs were everywhere in the Settlement, but there was no sign of any monsters. That wasn't enough to comfort anyone, since no one knew what had done this and so couldn't guess whether the things were crouching nearby and readying to strike. Judging by the shredded and mangled bodies, however, it became clear to Brett that whatever the cryptids were, they weren't doing this for food. Very little of the carcasses seemed to have been consumed, even if parts had been ripped off and flung blocks away. Thus, the things couldn't be sated enough not to kill, since they weren't doing it to get full.

This seemed like a preemptive attack meant as defense. To keep humans away from the underground world, whatever that world was? Or were they sicced on the unfortunate residents of Edinburgh of the Seven Seas by a human, whether Merco or the previous platoon of Organization-funded mercenaries? It didn't matter. Or, if it did matter, Brett wouldn't know until the creatures had set or been set upon them, and that would be too late to do anything about it except run.

After seeing dozens, maybe hundreds, of massacred humans and animals all through the Settlement, finally they reached the end of the badlands leading to the huge central peak. "I assume you know where this 'portal' is, Lathrop?"

The man bristled at the rude familiarity of Brett's address but was able to swallow it enough to say, "Yes, of course I do. We shall need transport, however, and the vehicles were lost in the sinking of the ship. Now, if you have some—"

A rumble and revving arose from about twenty feet away, and everyone turned to see Commander Crane's big face smiling out the right-side window of an open-backed ute. "Like Mister Rubble said, *Let's go!*"

Mister Rubble? Despite the doom around him, Brett had to smile, thinking, *He must be driving Lathrop out of his ever-lovin' mind.*

Lathrop climbed in next to Crane in the cab, and the rest of them piled into the back, ten of them in all plus some equipment and weapons they'd been able to salvage from the *Slangkop II*. The truck slowly made its way toward where they would enter this found world, and everyone with a gun kept it trained on the passing terrain lest some storybook monster launch a new attack at the fresh meat.

Nothing happened on the way, however. As they said in bad movies, everything was quiet—*too* quiet. No birds chirped or squawked on this lone spit of land in the center of hundreds of thousands of miles of open ocean. Nothing moved. Even the wind one would expect to incessantly batter an island like this was mostly absent. It was eerie, but not as eerie as the tremendous, monolithic volcano cone that grew and grew as they approached, finally blotting out half of the sky by the time they reached what Lathrop called *the portal*.

It was an ugly gash in a beautiful mountain. About sixty feet high, it was a seam with a fifty-foot-wide opening in the middle from fifteen feet up and closing after another twenty feet or so. It looked like a scar that refused to heal, Brett thought, but most of all it looked *unnatural*. If there was some kind of world underneath the island, it was never meant to be opened from this one. If this Doctor Merco is the one who did this so he could hide, then to hell with him; Brett had no problem turning over such a violator into the hateful clutches of the Organization.

Somehow, though, he felt this was the work of whatever knuckle-dragging Organization mercs were first sent in after the scientist. After all, Merco wanted to be sealed off, so he probably did so literally. He probably also was aware that allowing some kind of rabid monsters to escape and prey upon the outside world was a less than optimal action, but the commandos probably didn't even know *how* to close the mountain back up, regardless of whether they cared if the cryptids escaped or not.

He shrugged inwardly. It didn't matter now. This seam and apparently one opening into the ocean were open, allowing *things* to get out. What his group had to do now was watch its step very carefully, since the only weapons they had were light ones and the only ammo they had for them was what they carried with them, and hope they weren't set upon before they were able to get inside and then under the volcano.

"What did all this?" Ellie pondered out loud.

Popcorn, who walked while holding in front of him the backpack containing the solar-charging laptop he was able to grab from this ship, "I think the question is where are the things that did all this?"

Brett nodded. It was the question he and probably everyone else on the expedition had been asking themselves since they saw the bloody scenes along every street in the Settlement: as Popcorn said, where were the *things?*

A cry rang out behind and to Brett's left. He along with everyone else turned to see that one of the commandos—Falco, who sported a flattop haircut like a 1950s drill sergeant—had been staring at the imposing vista of the Tristan da Cunha volcano and fell into a depression in the earth about two feet deep. Perkins stood sheepishly and brushed himself off, then looked at what he had fallen into and said, "Holy cow. Commander, everybody—you want to take a look at this."

They sure did. Brett and Crane hurried over, the rest of the group letting the leaders do the leading. When they got there, Crane let out an impressed whistle and Brett felt his eyebrows go up in surprise.

Perkins was standing in the middle of a footprint. Not a pawprint—this was made by a *foot*. It didn't look human, since it was elongated with four short toes at the front and one out the side like a gorilla's foot. But Brett had seen plenty of gorilla footprints, and this looked like something in between a human's and a gorilla's.

That was interesting, but what floored Brett—and, he would guess by their silence, every other member of the party—was the size. The foot that made this print had to be six feet long: Crane was about 6' 5" and Brett guessed he could just about lie down inside the depression.

That meant, if this thing was proportioned like a human or an ape, it would be ...

"Thirty feet tall?" Popcorn said, his mathematical mind kicking in. "I think something with this size of a footprint, if it's bipedal and walks upright as an analog of humans or great apes, would have to be about thirty feet tall."

"That's impossible," Ravi the Mysterious Investigator replied, "and I don't say that about much."

"It might be possible, just barely. It would come in just at the very limit of what can exist on Earth given the cube-square law." He thought for a moment. "Depending on how deep this subterranean world goes, the giant might have evolved closer to the planet's core, where gravity isn't as strong. I'm hypothesizing and extrapolating here, of course."

"Of course," Ravi said, obviously blown away by the mental power of this African-American walking computer.

"Wouldn't we see something this huge walking around?" Ellie said.

Brett smiled. "That's what I thought, but there's a lot of this island we can't see blocked by the volcano. It also might have gone back down. But whatever it is, I don't think it's what tore all those people apart back there. That was the work of multiple animals, smaller than our King Kong here but probably bigger than panthers or other predators we know from the surface world."

"Whatever it is," Stefan said, never putting his camera down for fear of losing whatever amazing/horrifying thing might happen next for broadcast on *TMI*, "I think it might have scared everything else back down into the hole. I don't see anything moving here, not a single bird, much less any carnivorous monsters."

"Chased them back down? Like, into the hole we're about to go into?" Ravi said with a visible bobbing of his Adam's apple as he gulped.

"That's the plan," Brett answered, and motioned for them to get moving again. "There's a rise leading right into the portal there, and we're going to climb it and enter this found world. Get in, come out, avoid trouble in between."

~~~

The entrance to the passage under the island was tapered, narrowest at the start and then opening up as they went down the steep grade. There was nothing to see except the cross section of rock sheared off to make the passageway, and that was only until the light from the gash in the side of the mountain faded away. Brett didn't waste time thinking about who first created this access tunnel to the underground world or how they knew the place was underneath the volcano; he could ponder that later. But for right now, he was trying to lead the group he was starting to think of as "the castaways" through pitch blackness lit only by the flashlights of their phones, any useful things like flashlights or echolocators somewhere beneath the waves of the South Atlantic.

Something that gave Brett confidence that they would actually reach something at the end of this, however, was that the air was cooler than if this were a mine or just a very deep shaft. That meant fresh air, breathable air, lay in front of them. He knew a little geology along with his zoology and paleontology, and what he was experiencing flew in the face of all of it. Another lovely set of theories ruined by ugly facts.

"I see it!" Ellie gasped. "There *is* something down here!"

Brett enjoyed the feeling of the woman clutching onto his big arm. He had missed Ellie, but he wanted her to be safe … and life with him in the Amazon could never be safe. And the current situation *definitely* wasn't safe—but the difference was that he didn't bring her here. The Organization may have brought her on board because of Brett's involvement, but she had made the decision to go on this mission without knowing he would be there. Maybe she wouldn't have come if she had known. But the feeling of his ex-wife's skin on his did wonders for his disposition anyway.

What Ellie saw, and now Brett and the rest could see, was a glow that gradually strengthened as they continued down the slope of the widening tunnel. Wherever they were headed, it was well illuminated.

"That is eerie," Stefan said plainly, never moving the eyepiece of the camera away from its position in front of his right eye. "How can there be light? There's no sun down here."

Popcorn chimed in, "Bioluminescence. It's light produced by chemical interaction which releases a photon, or many photons, actually. I'd bet a dollar that it's bioluminescence down there."

"Ooh, a dollar." That was from the lantern-jawed commando, Leavitt, who said little, but when he did speak, it was usually something sarcastic or otherwise derisive.

"Do you smell that?" Ravi took a long inhale. "That humidity? I definitely smell plant life."

"That's not possible," Popcorn said. "The wavelengths of light produced by bioluminescence have been found insufficient to … um, fuel photo … um … photosynthesis …" His words trailed off as the exit to the long tunnel appeared, the steep grade flattening out to give them a straight-ahead view of the world they were about to enter.

It was a riot of foliage.

And yet another beautiful theory sent packing by inconvenient fact, Brett thought, and smiled. If nothing else, this would be an eye-opening adventure.

"Of course, there may be data suggesting otherwise," Popcorn finished weakly.

However, no one was listening to Popcorn now as they approached the dank-smelling jungle. The leafy plants and snaking vines looked like those above but weren't exact matches. Everything looked slightly *translated* down here, but one difference was dramatic and, as they all saw as they reached the threshold, completely pervasive.

The plants were blue.

They were a pale blue, almost blue-green, but not quite. It gave an impression of unreality, like they were in a Vegas casino that had created an alien planet as an attraction for tourists. Also, Brett could hear weird calls of what he assumed were birds, although the sound could have been any kind of animal, he supposed; but whatever they were, they didn't exist up top. And, for the moment, they were hidden from view, and that put Brett on full alert. If they could see you but you couldn't see them, then they had a distinct advantage.

They stepped past the threshold and for the first time saw the "sky" above, which glowed with blue light, giving it the appearance of its terrestrial analog but without a distinct "sun."

"It don't look real," the burly commando called Junior said, reaching out and feeling the flat leaf of a squat subterranean plant.

"Don't touch anything!" Brett snapped—but it was too late.

The leaf quivered for a second at the contact, then like lightning wrapped around Junior's hand and forearm. Junior screamed with shock, then laughed. "Sorry, that was girly! But it does got a good grip on me. Gimme a hand, guys? Heh, a hand, get it?"

Junior's levity relaxed the situation, which was good because Commander Crane and all three of the other mercs had spun to train their assault weapons on the weird blue flora. Stefan had turned the camera toward Junior and Brett had his machete out and raised so fast that no one had time to realize they hadn't noticed Brett even had such a weapon on his person.

"Stay still," Brett said to Junior, motioning for the commandos to stand down as he approached with the huge blade.

"It's just a stupid plant. I bet I can …" he wriggled, trying to free his hand, but to no avail. "It's got me pretty good, guys."

"I said say still." Brett was almost there, moving very carefully. "Some plants up top grab meat and dissolve it with acid. We don't know what this thing can do."

"This ain't a Venus Flytrap, Hoss," Junior said. "And I ain't no fly, okay?" He pulled again against the tight grip the plant had on him.

Brett reached him and grabbed his arm to keep him from yanking back anymore. He said sternly but quietly to the big lummox, "Goddamn, listen to me: *stay still*. I'm going to chop it at the—"

The smile slid off Junior's face. "It's getting warm all of a sudden. Kinda hot, actually." By the time Brett had raised the machete, the commando was already shrieking in pain and panic. "*Get it off me! God, get it off me! GOD!*"

The machete came down swiftly and lopped the leaf off right where it grew off the branch. Junior fell backward onto his ass, the leaf still wrapped tightly around his paw despite his using his hands and then booted feet to strip it off.

No one noticed that, however, since the branch where Brett chopped off the leaf sputtered and leaked onto the ground, sizzling into the soil.

"It has acid for blood?" Crane said, as dumbstruck as the rest of the contingent, including the smooth Lathrop and his female agent who had hung far back and let the hired help do the exploring and possibly dying.

"Plants don't have blood," Popcorn said in his casually pedantic manner. "They rely upon 'chains' of phloem to bring sugars and other metabolic—"

"*Quiet*," Brett barked, and the black nerd stopped like he'd been shot in the head.

Once everyone had processed the *Alien*-level biological surprise, they noticed that Junior the commando was still screaming, now writhing around on the ground and struggling desperately to slough off the death-grip wrap of the leaf on his hand. "*Help me! Holy god, it BURNS!*"

Brett stepped over and knelt down, then motioned to the man's fellow mercenaries. "Hold him down and keep him still," he ordered, and none of them protested that he wasn't the boss of them, one advantage of dealing with toy soldiers instead of actual military, Brett thought.

What Brett really didn't want to see—aside from a freaking *acid plant* as soon as they stepped through the door—was Junior stop struggling and lie still, a million beads of sweat lying on his clammy skin. The commando was going into shock.

What the hell IS this place? Brett's mind shouted at him, but he focused his attention on the job in front of him. There would be plenty of time for *WTF?* later.

He hoped.

He shook that off and leaned down to take a close look at the leaf around Junior's hand. The wrap was turning black now, and it smelled sickeningly like a pig roast. There wasn't going to be anything left of the man's right hand and half his forearm. Even if they could somehow get the thing off him—and when Brett tried to lift a corner to peel it away, it was like touching a frying pan full of sizzling and popping oil—it would be worse than useless, but a massive target for infection, and Brett had the feeling all the antibiotics and other first aid items had gone down with the ship.

So, before anyone could protest, he lifted the machete again and brought it down half an inch away from where the plant was wrapped on his arm. Junior howled and then passed out, blood starting to pump from his arm. Everyone else shouted or screamed as well, but Brett ignored them, stripped off the long-sleeve shirt he wore loose over his tee, and made a tight tourniquet that stopped the bleeding immediately.

"Congratulations, Nurse Russell," Lathrop mocked, stepping forward now that the danger seemed to have passed. "We now have an invalid. He will surely be grateful when he awakes in riotous pain for which we have no relief and finds himself alone in an alien world."

"Alone?" Crane said in confusion. "His legs aren't hurt, sir. When he wakes up, we'll just—"

"Just what? Bring a dazed, useless man along with us to slow everything down? I think not." And with that, Lathrop drew a Luger from a shoulder holster beneath his expensive but ruined suit and shot the unconscious man literally right between the eyes.

Everyone jumped at the *crack* of the gun, including Brett three inches from the line of fire. But it wasn't just the humans: the unmistakable flapping of wings large and small accompanied the shrieks of strange birds and other creatures as they leapt into the air in surprise and possibly fright.

Brett leapt to his feet and stepped up to Lathrop with murder in his own eyes. "You dumb son of a bitch! You just alerted every goddamn monster in this place to our presence! And you killed a man who *did not need to die!*"

Lathrop raised the Luger so it pointed at Brett's ripped stomach. "He wouldn't have been of much use to us even as a decoy, Mister Russell. And don't think I will hesitate to shoot you dead or worse. Now I suggest, as you people say, that you step off. Killing you would be counterproductive to our mission … but I am willing to do it and put Commander Crane in your place."

Brett seethed but stood down. He untied the tourniquet—he'd need any protection possible in this hyper-hostile environment, and poor Junior didn't need it anymore. The commando was dead and there was no point in throwing the baby out with the bathwater over him. But damn, he hated Lathrop the Organization weasel. "All right, we'll play this out. But we need to move from this location, and right now. Too many things know we're—"

"No. Oh, *hell*, no," Flattop the commando said, stepping backward away from whatever he was looking at on the ground.

Brett spun around and saw what was freaking out an actual trained mercenary killer, and it made him involuntarily back up as well. It took less than five seconds for everyone in the troupe to see it for themselves, and to a person they immediately and totally instinctively put another five to ten feet between them and it.

Junior had been dead for less than two minutes, but that was apparently enough for the fresh meat to be detected. But not by insects or animals—by other *plants*.

Vines had crept out and now encircled the dead man, squeezing him right and raising smoke wherever they were in contact with flesh. They were acidic as well. Then, like muscles contracting, the vines stiffened and, impossibly, slowly dragged Junior into the thick foliage until no one could see it anymore.

"I'm out," Ravi said, and turned to go back to the tunnel.

But his partner stopped him. "No you don't," Stefan said, camera still glued to his eye, his arm extended to halt Ravi without him even looking at anything but the frame that the dead commando had just been dragged out of. "I'm getting every second of this on video, and the storage media stayed nice and dry in the case with the camera. We got *days* of memory space, man—this is gonna put *TMI* on the map. You *cannot* back out now. We need you, me, and Ellie. All of us."

Ravi looked at Ellie. "We're not going to be famous if we're frickin' *dead*, come on."

"I'm not going anywhere," Ellie said, and Brett hoped he was a little bit of the reason for that. Then he stopped and chided himself: *That is not why she's here.* Then added, a bit more harshly, *Or why you are, either, pal.*

When he called himself "pal," he knew he had let his thoughts go to places they shouldn't. He *hated* being called "pal," and only used it on people he was fed up with. Including, in this instance, himself.

"Unfortunate," Lathrop said with an insincere-looking shake of his head. "However, an acceptable loss. Let us keep moving—keep our eyes on the prize, yes?"

Brett stared at him and muttered, "Whatever you say, pal."

~~~

There was a path between the blue leaves, some fern-like, others broad like the one that had attacked Junior, some splayed out like maple leaves, and every member of Brett's party stuck right to the middle of it. At both edges of the path were scorched ends of plants; the earlier Organization troop must have burned their way through. This was helpful in moving through the terrain without being dissolved by a thousand brushes against the plant life, but it wouldn't do to just follow where the others had gone. They were most likely dead, eaten by God knew what, and Brett wasn't anxious for them to follow that example.

He looked around at this complete underground ecosystem. The sky was that bioluminescent blue, making everything look unreal. Maybe it was the teal foliage, too, but everything was dreamlike ... or maybe nightmarish, considering what just the *plants* were like.

"Mister Russell?" Popcorn called, mincing around people to get to the front of their single-file line while avoiding the edges of the killer vegetation. "I have an alarming thought."

"Oh, goody."

"Actually, it is to complete a previous alarming thought: I realized that these plants exhibiting ... um, *carnivorous* characteristics is a logical outgrowth of this sky's bioluminescence being insufficient for photosynthesis. I'd wager the plants down here evolved from ancestors in the surface world, making a transition from photosynthesis to gleaning energy from consuming meat. That's how the acid developed; the Venus Flytrap is our best-known carnivorous plant, and it uses acid to digest its—"

"Okay, that's plenty," Brett said. "That's disgusting, but how is that any more alarming? We know the things want to eat us. Knowing why makes it at least make sense."

"That's not what I mean is alarming. What I mean is that, if these plants get energy from consuming insect and animal flesh, then there must be plentiful animals here, enough to feed every plant we see and a lot we don't."

"And some of those animals might be hungry themselves. For, say, the catch of the day, a bunch of humans."

Popcorn nodded but then shook his head. "Not *some* of the animals. Unless they have some kind of magic ability not to be burned by acid—and they *don't*, because the plants wouldn't be able to eat them—*all they eat is meat*. That means that every plant, insect, and animal here wants to kill us and eat us … and not necessarily in that order."

The final commando, Todd, with a shaved head and a tattoo above his left ear that said ALWAYS FIGHING (sadly, not FIGHTING) must have heard this, because he abruptly stopped walking and actually stomped his foot as he said, "This is BULL! We could *die* down here!"

Everyone's eyes darted to the others. To Brett, Ellie mouthed the words, *What the hell?*

Brett tried to tamp down a smile and failed. After a moment, he recovered his composure and said to Lathrop, "Some real West Point valedictorians you got there."

"*Crane!* Get your man together, for Christ's sake!"

Brett thought Commander Crane may have been as stunned as anyone at hearing the words coming out of Todd's mouth, but he was able to shake himself out of it, took three steps back in line to get to the merc, and punched him straight in the face. Todd fell, but wasn't knocked out. He felt his bloody nose, looked up at his boss, and nodded that he needed the attitude adjustment. "Sorry, everyone," Todd said like someone arriving late to a meeting. "Got a little extra freaked out there."

Brett looked at Lathrop, this time smiling, narrowing his eyes, and cocking his head to say, *Really?*

Lathrop ignored him and said to Crane, "As enchanting as Soldier of Fortune Day Care is, Commander, I'd prefer if we got moving before the meat-eating plants—"

"Quiet," Brett said sharply, and everyone stopped speaking or moving at his command. He took a slow look around them: there were hills in the near distance, and they looked bare of the blue-green foliage. Possibly animals didn't venture up there for fear of being eaten by things that flew. In that case, the plants couldn't survive there. Also, it would make a good lookout place, something they needed since Brett had no idea where to go within this vast underground world other than to follow the path burned open by the earlier mission's flamethrowers.

Man, he wished they had flamethrowers.

He wished that more than ever because what prompted him to silence everyone was a distinct *buzz* wavering in the still air. There were no airborne insects pestering them or flying near anyone's ears … which was bad. That meant the *buzz* was coming from a distance, and *that* meant it was big enough that Brett could hear it flying from this far away.

"Something's coming," he said to the group.

Everyone seemed to hear what he was talking about at the same time. Each person whirled around, stopped, turned some more, stopped again, trying to pinpoint the direction the sound was coming from. But there was no way to locate the source … because the buzzing was coming from every direction at once.

This, too, seemed to dawn on everyone at the same time. "We can't take cover under the trees, can we? The trees could eat us," Ravi said, looking longingly at the taller trees just off the scorched path. He pointed at the same clutch of hills that Brett had been sizing up. "There's a bald patch on the top of that rise. No plants there."

"But they'd pick us off easy there," his partner Stefan countered, sounding a bit panicked. His audio earpiece for the camera amplified the *buzz* maddeningly. "We can't be up high and exposed like that."

Now Brett could see black splotches skimming above the low plants and zipping around the taller trees. They came from several directions, although not from where the hills were. Since the low mountains looked like they would take hours to reach on foot, the hills seemed like the only differentiated area in sight. They were definitely on the menu just standing out there, so a chance was better than nothing. "That way, to the hills, *now*," he said in a voice brooking no argument and moved swiftly in that direction, putting his hands up into the sleeves of his shirt stained with blood from the dead commando. He adjusted the rest of his clothing, too, anything to repel incidental acidic contact as they made a dash off the path and through the plant life to get to the hills and, maybe, avoid being attacked by whatever those things were making that ungodly sound. A sound which was growing steadily louder, as the whatever-they-were were definitely coming directly at them. "Fine," he said to Stefan, "you stay here. The rest of you, *move!*" He took Ellie's hand and started running.

"I didn't mean it like that!" Stefan managed to say while joining the troupe in a sprint for the hills, his camera finally not up to his eye for a minute.

The commandos were already well covered in their tactical gear, but the rest of them were busy covering their exposed arms with anything they were wearing that could do the job. Even still, the reek of burning fabric enveloped them as they dashed off the trail and through the killer plants if there was going to be any possibility of safety ahead.

All of them ran practically on the balls of their feet as they danced and darted to avoid the touch of the low-lying leaves, making small zig-zags and letting out an "ow!" or other cries of surprise and pain as they moved as fast as they could to cover the half-mile to the nearest hill. Brett had to let go of Ellie's hand, since not having the ability to maneuver as well around the plants did more harm than keeping her up with him was doing good.

They were still hundreds of feet from the hill—and who knew if there would by any safety there once they reached it—when the *buzz* became so loud Brett had to turn to see what was happening. "Oh, *hell*," he said out loud.

The things that were buzzing out of the sky were giant wasps. Or maybe not exactly wasps, but damned close except that they looked like they were made of brushed gray metal instead of the black of their terrestrial cousins. It made them look like alien robots—alien robots with enormous wings and stingers, that was. Their compound eyes were the same gunmetal color as the rest of them, giving them a horrible, unreal quality.

But they were real. The first of the fifty or more that Brett could see closing in dove at Flattop, the commando bringing up the rear of the group. It didn't bring its massive stinger to bear on him, instead barreling into him from behind and knocking him down hard into the soil. It then made a high loop that completed with the *ur*-wasp swooping down low and grabbing Flattop with serrated claws at the end of its legs. It was then that Brett and the others could see the full scale of the monsters: the one that had singled out Flattop was at least half again as long as the six-foot man. It was like an unpainted midsize sedan has flown down to pick him off from the group, lifting him and his heavy bag of weapons.

But it didn't sting him. Neither that giant bug nor its dozens of compatriots stung anyone. But more were coming in low now, maybe to sting, but more likely to carry more of them off—to what end, Brett didn't want to think about. "*Run!*" he shouted, but Ravi and Stefan rushed past him before he could even turn back around to run himself.

Pop! Pow!

Everyone reflexively looked up at the source of the gunshots and saw Flattop put another round through the thorax of the enormous wasp, which sent them spiraling down together into the brush one hundred feet away.

"They can die! Let's help 'em get there!" Crane hollered, and he and the two other commandos yanked assault rifles out of their own zipped weapon bags and started blasting the other mega-wasps. *Blam!* The closest one lost its wing and whirled at them like a kamikaze fighter plane hit by anti-aircraft fire.

Ellie was stopped in front of Brett, frozen in place at the sight of the giant insect hurtling toward them. At the last second, Brett grabbed her arm and jumped with her out of the way just before the wasp smashed into the ground and made a fifty-foot-long furrow before it stopped.

Brett found himself on his back with Ellie up against him. It felt nice, but as soon as each of them noticed the other one noticing them enjoying it, they sprang up and brushed the soil off themselves without making further eye contact.

"I'm okay!" Flattop yelled from where he had crashed enveloped in the now-dead bug, lugging his weapons bag and carrying the AK-47 as he ran to them, skirting the dangerous plants all the way. "Boy, I thought those things were ugly from far away! They're even worse close up."

Crane laughed and said, "Thank God that's ov—"

Clicketyclacketyclicketyclackety

There was a strange and very loud moist clicking sound from behind the hill and those facing it lost all color as they saw what was making the noise: a phalanx of jet-black centipedes—each with a body as long as a city bus and slimy antenna reached out like a handlebar moustache over their oversized mandibles, which also happened to be loaded with dagger-like fangs—slithered over the crest and started down toward them at alarming speed.

Everyone was completely paralyzed with fear, including Brett, but he was able to count the number of creatures coming to devour them in an extremely painful manner. There were ten of them—one for each survivor. There were ten people left in the group, he believed, but counted everyone off just in case—Brett, Ellie, Popcorn, Ravi, Stefan, Lathrop, the Organization woman, Commander Crane, and his three surviving commandos Flattop, Todd, and Todd. That made eleven, not ten.

Oh, yeah, Brett thought sheepishly, *I forgot about Leavitt*. He was focusing too much on Ellie, he knew it, to the point where he wasn't even aware of how many people were on his expedition.

There were going to be a lot fewer of them in about twenty seconds if he didn't get them all away from the titanic centipedes—*megapedes*, Brett named them automatically— rushing at them. It occurred to him that he didn't know how megapedes killed their prey, so it was hard to know what to do except try to escape their path.

"Avoid those jaws!" Ravi shouted as he and Stefan ran back past Brett the other way.

"No kidding," Flattop said.

"No, I mean once a centipede gets you into its jaws, they inject you with poison! *You don't want that!*"

As Brett joined the rest in running the opposite direction they had wanted—they were now putting as much distance between themselves and the hill as humanly possible—he noticed thin lines of smoke rose from where each of the wasps had gone down over a hundred-yard arc in the foliage. Brett could feel his brain making some kind of connection, but it wasn't until he saw a coil of rope flopping around inside Crane's open weapons bag that he came to it.

"Commander—why do you have rope?"

"For the grappling hooks, duh." He actually said *duh*.

But his answer was exactly what Brett was hoping for. He yelled at the top of his lungs, "*Everybody! Make for the wasp in the middle!*" and punctuated his command by running through and ahead of the group so they could follow him to the one he meant. The acid bites from jutting leaves barely registered as their adrenaline pumped to keep them running faster than the glistening, hundred-plus-legged creatures articulating over the hill and onto the ground after them.

They did. But Popcorn, who was not a runner under the best circumstances, was huffing and puffing as he tried and failed to keep up with the rest of the group. The megapede that was racing at the front of the pack was almost to the obese black nerd, its jaws opening in preparation for the big meal. Brett knew that if Popcorn fell into the thing's mandible, he'd be shot full of poison and die an agonizing and terrifying death. Even if the man was going to slow them down, Brett wasn't going to just let a member of his team die. Besides, although they didn't have any tech right now, Lathrop wouldn't have brought someone on board whose expertise he didn't expect them to need.

Except Ellie, maybe. Her "expertise" in Lathrop's eyes may just have been to keep Brett motivated. But she was a fine adventurer in her own right, and the fact that she was here with a team from a show about cryptids and other paranormal phenomena told him that she had never given up the *Cryptids Alive!* curiosity and spirit that had gotten them together in the first place.

But right now he needed to save Orville Blum. The lead megapede was just about on top of him, and Popcorn was doing that thing where you simultaneously look behind you as the thing gets nearer and slow down because you're looking behind yourself instead of where you're going. This was going to get Popcorn devoured before Brett could do what he needed to do. "*Popcorn! Hit the afterburners, man!*"

Popcorn nodded, mouth open as he gasped for air to fuel a little more running, if possible with a little more speed. He performed admirably—but not quite well enough, as the megapede was going to get to him before Brett got to the large tree he was running toward with the rope and grappling hook. He needed to be able to shoot the hook around the only other big tree within the rope's range, but first he had to get the gun itself secured—

"*Help! Hurry up, please!*" Popcorn screamed, polite even unto his awful doom.

Brett muttered quite the series of curse words as he realized there was no time to secure the hook's rifle within a tree on his end. He had to fire *now* if he was going to get the rope across in time. So he took the shot.

The hook and rope exploded away from the rifle, shot across the middle area where Popcorn and the megapede were about to cross, and whipped around the trunk of Brett's target tree.

"*Yes!*" Brett shouted and pumped his first. But now came the hard part: he looped the remaining rope around himself with the body of the rifle behind him. Then he took a deep breath and steeled every muscle. He would have to be the other tree now if this was going to work, and he believed it was going to hurt quite a bit.

However, it hurt Popcorn first. He had only two seconds or so to see that a thick rope had been stretched across the lane where he was running from the monster, but it was enough time for him to jump to clear it. Unfortunately, the highest jump that the fat and exhausted indoor kid could make didn't provide the two feet of clearance he needed. He leapt, but both his ankles caught the rope and he was hurled into the ground, luckily face-planting where there wasn't a broad-leafed acid plant ready to eat his face. He slid on his face for a few feet, then immediately started crawling forward without even stopping to get the caked soil off his glasses.

Those couple of feet were vital, because when the first megapede hit the wire, it took its first half-dozen legs out from under it and it too, face-planted into the dirt. But only a couple of feet, because most of it stayed behind the rope, stopping it completely.

When the thing hit the rope, Brett had to dig his heels into the dirt like he was competing in the world's toughest game of tug of war. The impact wrenched his back and almost threw him to become the third face-plant of the day, but he was able to keep his body tight, bending back almost flat to offer the greatest amount of resistance. He couldn't grab any of the sturdy-looking shrubs or the tree he had originally wanted to tie the rope around because they'd burn his hands at best and probably eat them like they did Junior's. So he used the ground to help him resist the brute *yank* of the tripping megapede.

In the moment after the monster tripped but before the next ones slammed into it, Brett was able to regain his footing and sprint around the huge tree on his side, using the rifle itself as a lock to keep the loop closed. An instant after he let go of the rifle, the tree was mightily squeezed by the force of the second, then third and fourth, and then the rest of the megapedes running into the backs of the ones that had already stopped.

Brett smelled smoke, or at least some kind of vapor from something burning. It smelled like leaves burning in the fall. He looked at the tree with the rope around it and saw that the acid was eating through the fibers of the rope.

Aw, hell. He saw that the rest of the group had just about made it to the smoldering wasp carcass in the middle and that Popcorn had regained his legs and was doing his best to speed-walk there as well. This was good, because the megapedes in back were already trying to move around the pileup, and once the rope burned through, all of them would be able to come after the group again. He ran like a demon to join the rest of them, shouting, *"Get behind the wasp! Guys, open fire when they get close! Go!"*

The ten other survivors of the expedition did just what he said, with Crane and his three commandos peering over the top a few seconds after they all dove behind the long and thick carcass. Brett could see them hacking the nearby plants away with machetes.

They have machetes? I'm going to kill them, Brett thought, but that could wait, given that four AK-47 muzzles were pointed at him— really *past* him since he was between the commandos and the megapedes, but it didn't feel like a safe place to think bad things about the mercenaries right then.

He didn't have to look back to know that the rope had snapped and that the monsters were approaching again: every person looking over the dead mega-wasp jerked in reflex at the same time, and the commandos lined up their eyes with the sights of their weapons. The rope trick had been done about 150 feet from the wasp, and Brett was now about twenty feet from the rest of the group. That meant the fast-moving things would probably be about 100 feet away by the time

Brett was able to get out of the line of fire. Could the rent-a-soldiers actually do something right? Could they take out ten enormous killer cryptids in the fifteen or so seconds before the things would be upon them again?

Brett got there and fell to the ground in front of the wasp barrier; he'd crawl around to get behind it, but those bastards needed to get shooting *now*.

Which they did: in real life, nobody goes "rock and roll" with submachine guns. It wastes an amazing amount of ammo and provides less accuracy than aiming and firing, then firing again, each shot distinct. The fact that the Organization paramilitary soldiers did this made Brett feel a little less doomed about the mission.

Pow! Pow! Pow! Pow! Pow! The four guns cracked with shot after shot, and the squeals and shrieks from the huge creatures was music to his ears, even as he kept his palms flat against them to keep from going deaf from the dozens, then hundreds of shots a few feet away.

The megapedes had size on their side when it came to attacking, but that very hugeness were there undoing here: as each shell slammed into their membrane-wrapped gel, the entire body of the victim tried to curl around the injury, the pain cramping their bodies around wherever they were hit. This stopped their forward motion almost immediately, and the more shots the commandos landed, the further each megapede closed in upon itself. The shooters weren't ready to stop, however; they kept firing until the things stopped moving entirely. Even then, each man took a couple of extra shots just to remind this underworld nightmare realm who was boss.

Brett gave a thumbs-up and yelled, "Good shootin', boys!"

Brett couldn't hear his own words or anything else, but he saw a strange look on Commander Crane's face and could read the words on his lips: *No way*.

Brett looked and saw what Crane must have been affected by: vines extended from the plants next to the massive bug corpses and started feeding. The sizzling sound was unmistakable, and soon the acrid stench would reach them as well. Everybody in the group saw it and gagged or looked beyond horrified or both.

"Hey," Popcorn said through his still-heavy breathing, "why aren't the plants eating this thing?" He was looking at the body of wasp, which had been singed by the acid of the plants it had landed on, but for which no vines had been extended. The plants that the commandos hadn't cleared away with the machetes may have ended up touching the carcass just by the lay of their leaves, but other than a small scorch mark at the point of contact, the potential meal was entirely ignored.

"That's interesting," Ellie said.

It was more than interesting to Brett. "Guys, let's drag all the wasps over here. We can make a little fort so we can decide what to do next without being eaten by death plants."

"*Drag* them? They have to weigh a ton! Like, literally," Ravi said, looking distressed. He spent a lot of time in the field for *TMI*, but none of it had involved physical labor. At his comment, everyone looked at Brett. The commandos may have had the guns, Lathrop and the Organization woman may have had the power, but Brett was the one who everyone looked to for answers. This was how it should be for the leader of an expedition, but Brett didn't know if he had ever led one so full of helpless people.

Brett considered this for a moment, then said to Crane, "You have three more grappling hooks, right?"

"Yep."

"Great. Why don't you guys take your *four goddamn machetes* and cut down some of the plants between here and the other wasps so we can get to them without being burned by the plants, okay? And why the hell didn't you use the machetes before? We're all injured here."

Crane shrugged. "Didn't think of it for plants. We usually just use 'em on people, so it was outside of our usual schema, y'know?"

Schema? Brett echoed in his mind. Crane was like an idiot savant, but without much savant. All he said was, "Naturally. Maybe your three men could do that and you hang here with your gun trained on any new friends who might come to say hello."

"That's what I was going to command them just now," Crane said, which was definitely not true but was hardly worth arguing about to Brett right then.

For the moment, at least, there were no new assaults. (Except on their senses, as the plants made an unholy stank as they consumed the ninety-foot-long line of dead megapedes.) Crane's men cleared paths between the giant insect they hid behind and the four others, which the commandos found before the carcasses ceased smoldering. The deadly plants really didn't seem to care about the gunmetal-colored cryptids, a fact that Brett filed away for later.

Now Brett marshaled everyone except Stefan, who insisted that he stay with the camera in front of him to record everything that happened. Brett had Crane give Stefan a powerful sidearm so the Mysterious Investigator could at least stand guard. Then Brett told everyone his plan: "We don't know why, but these crazy plants won't touch the wasp bodies. That means that we can use the wasps as barriers against the plants. What we're going to do is drag all of the wasps over here and make a square we can all sit inside while we figure out what to do next."

"That's five wasps," Popcorn said. "Really, we just need to drag three of the corpses over here to complete the square with the one we have."

"Don't worry about that. I have plans for the last one."

"Indeed? My apologies."

"Don't worry about that, either," Brett said, and split them into two groups of three and one of four. The four-person group was made up of Flattop, Todd, Popcorn, and Ravi, since the two civilians were pretty weak physically compared to the others and would need two strong commandos. Crane, Brett, and Ellie made up the second team, with Leavitt and the Organization villains Lathrop and the woman making up the third. While he was at it, Brett decided to ask his burning question: "Lathrop, I can't keep calling your partner there 'the Organization woman.' What's her name?"

"Natasha," the woman said with a probably fake Russian accent and a definitely genuine smirk that told Brett just where he could stick his questions. "I vant to keel moose and squirrel."

"Cute. Well, you and Boris go with Leavitt. What we're going to do is have each soldier shoot a grappling hook into or around a wasp, then all of you drag it back here. Once we have those three in place, Crane and his boys can go back for the last one. Understood?"

They understood, even if not one of the civilians liked the idea. That was too damn bad for them, in Brett's opinion. They had gotten here with only one casualty, even though they had just a tiny fraction of the firepower they were supposed to have and no idea where Doctor Merco and his superweapon might be. There hadn't even been any sign of the earlier extraction mission, which made Brett wonder if there weren't some very well-fed acid plants somewhere in the vicinity. Plants that probably just couldn't wait to have another meal of human flesh.

With the paths cleared, the job of dragging the massive insect bodies was only very hard, not actually injurious. Sweating like crazy—the underground world was as humid as the Amazon rainforest, even without a hot sun beating down on them—each team managed to get its carcass to where Stefan stood filming it all and put it into position to make three-foot-high walls of a nine-by-nine square fort. Then the commandos went back and got the last wasp, sliding it to a spot a few feet away from the little encampment and then getting themselves inside the protected area. Now eleven people sat jammed together with their backs against the creepy dead-wasp walls. Maybe they were safer this way or maybe a predator could just swoop in or climb over and get them, but it definitely felt great to everyone there to sit down and take a couple of deep and calming breaths.

But that was all there was time for. Brett was not thrilled that the dumbass mercenaries forgot they have freaking *machetes* with them while they were all trying to dance around plants that wanted only to burn, dissolve, and consume them. So he said, "All right, fellas, I need to know what every person on this expedition is carrying on them. Everyone, put your stuff in the center. Empty out the bags, turn out your pockets, everything in the middle so I can see what the hell we have to fight through this place."

There was a bit of grumbling, but Crane ordered his men to do as Brett said, and everyone else except Lathrop and Natasha followed his instructions. Inside the bags each of the commandos had managed to salvage off the ship—luckily, their orders were to never allow them out of their sight, so they were right at hand—were one AK-47 submachine gun, two Baretta M9s pistols, five MK3A2 concussion grenades, two M67 fragmentation grenades, one grappling hook with one hundred feet of coiled rope, six MREs, a machete, a pair of binoculars, one huge serrated tactical knife, one huge non-serrated tactical knife, a first-aid tin, one small LED flashlight and one large one, and three hard-plastic water bottles. So they had four times that much in total now.

The rest of them had wallets, pocket knives, electronic equipment, video memory cards, pens, cell phones, and a bunch of other stuff that wouldn't help them much at all. Brett threw in his satchel of belongings, the nontrivial contents of which were the only marginally more helpful compass, waterproof matches, tranq gun, and, ironically, bug repellent. He assumed everyone could see the bowie knife and flashlight on his belt.

"This is what we got to work with, people," Brett said, waving off the expression of protest that immediately showed on Crane's face at his and his commandos' property suddenly belonging to *us*. "Don't worry, Commander—everything's going back to the people who brought it. I just want to know what we can depend on if we need it … whatever the hell that need might look like."

They all replaced the items in their bags, satchels, and pockets. Then they sat there for a while and looked at the weird blue sky without a sun.

Finally, Stefan turned the camera on Brett and Ellie asked in her interviewer voice, "We just got attacked by killer plants, giant wasps, and monster centipedes. How much more do you think we'll face before we find Doctor Merco, Mister Russell?"

Mister Russell? "You're really doing this right now?" Brett said, less annoyed than just feeling the adrenaline seep away.

"That's why Mister Lathrop brought us on board," Ellie said.

Brett exchanged a look with Lathrop, whose expression showed that they both knew this wasn't why his ex-wife just happened to be there. It was leverage, pure and simple, but Brett would rather be eaten by a megapede than embarrass his beloved Ellie. So he said, "All right, let me enlighten the viewers of *Inside The Mystery* —"

"*The Mysterious Investigators*," Ravi corrected like he was quite used to people completely butchering the title. "Just remember: it's *TMI*."

"It sure is," Brett said with a smirk, but then got down to answering the question: "We're at a real disadvantage here. We don't know where this scientist is or where the earlier team is, or even if they're still alive. Every single element of this environment is hostile to humans, to say the least. We don't have any gear beyond basic defense and survival. And without a sun, it's almost impossible to keep track of direction or what time it might be. Is there night here? If there is, maybe we'll be able to see cooking fires or whatever Merco uses to light where he lives down here. *If* he lives at all."

"Very dramatic," Ravi said. "Nice."

Brett gave him a quizzical look. "Ellie's the host, Stefan is the cameraman—what do *you* do, Ravi?"

Sitting up straighter, Ravi said with dignity, "I am the producer."

"What does that mean?"

"I ... it means ... it means I produce the show! Make sure everything is in place for capturing footage, getting Ellie to stand in front of things, all that sort of stuff. Basically, I make the show *happen*."

"Gotcha. So I'm like the producer of this little expedition, making things happen if they're going to happen at all."

"I suppose so."

"Like if people have *goddamn machetes* that could help us cut through a whole mile of acid-oozing *killer plants*, I have to *remind* them, for instance."

"Hey!" Crane said with feathers ruffled. "Are you talking about us?"

"No, of course not," Brett said, his anger having the chance to surface now that they were out of immediate danger. "I'm talking about the *other* idiots who almost got all of us killed."

Crane relaxed. "Oh, okay, good."

"So Lathrop was the casting agent, and I'm the producer," Brett said, then came around to what he really wanted to ask. He turned his gaze to Natasha. "And what's your story? The Organization needed two weasels here?"

Natasha replied by saying something very unladylike, indeed.

Brett laughed. "Yeah, I didn't really expect an answer."

"Why don't you concentrate on getting Doctor Merco instead of trying to get information you wouldn't even understand, Mister Russell?" Lathrop said. "How is the producer of *The Found World* going to get his cast and crew to find the real star of the show?"

"Fine." Brett sat up straighter himself, took out his big Bowie knife, and drew a small square in the dirt in the center of their tiny encampment. "This is us, right here. My compass doesn't work down here—maybe Popcorn can tell me why—so I'm going to call the mountain we can see from here 'north.'" He drew a peak and an N at one edge of the cleared soil and continued, "I think this is the best candidate for where someone could hole up for an extended period of time against the monsters and killer *everything* here. These are mountains underneath a volcano, so maybe Doctor Merco was able to find a cave within a mountain under a mountain, if you get me."

"Those mountains are also far from the portal, so anybody coming for Merco would have to trek through all of this horrible place," Ellie added.

"Exactly. There are some hills, lots of forest and low-lying vegetation, but that mountain is singular. Plus what Ellie said, all of this says to me that the only thing to do is go north. I bet that if we can get to the mountain, we'll find Merco and maybe the earlier mission, too."

"I don't know," Ravi said. "It seems like the further we get from the portal, the nastier the monsters become. Acid plants are bad, but giant wasps are worse, and bus-sized centipedes are even worse than that."

"What do you suggest we do, then?"

"Maybe cut our losses and head back. We have a whole season's worth of footage already."

"You ignorant ass!" Lathrop cut in. "We're not here for your ridiculous program! The only reason you're even part of this mission is because of Ellie White in the first place."

"What?" Ravi said, looking completely befuddled. Stefan shared his confusion, even taking his eye away from the camera for a moment. Ellie's mouth hung agape.

"For God's sake, Lathrop, you brought my ex-wife as bait to get me here?" Brett scoffed, but immediately realized that he didn't know she was coming until they were almost to the island. "No, not *bait* … then what?"

"Insurance," Lathrop said. "Now, enough of this monkeyshines. Mister Russell, how are we to get to the mountain in one piece? I doubt that giant bugs or evil greenery took apart every last living thing in Edinburgh of the Seven Seas. Whatever did that—not to mention sea monsters—could lie in wait for us. I hired you because I was told you always have a plan and, like a Canadian Mountie, you always get your man. Or cryptid or what have you. Hmm, Scout Leader, are you prepared? Do you, in fact, have a plan?"

Of *course* he didn't have a plan, except to work through whatever obstacles were necessary to get to Doctor Merco and retrieve his reward from Lathrop, and even that plan was complicated beyond reason by losing ninety percent of their mission supplies when the boat sank. But saying that might inspire some dissention in the ranks, and they were fractured enough already. "I just told you the plan. We go north to the mountain. When we get to the scientist, we put him in cuffs, ransack his supplies, and then use whatever safe method of travel he used to get to the mountain in the first place, only we use it to come back across this place to get to the portal and get the hell back to the surface. Then the Organization sends a boat or choppers or whatever and gets off Tristan da Cunha and back to Cape Town, where you pay every one of us or I will kill you with my bare hands."

Popcorn, who had finally caught his breath from trying to run a hundred yards, put his hand on Brett's shoulder and said solemnly to Lathrop, "And he won't be alone."

Brett closed his eyes. He literally couldn't have created a less-threatening person than Orville Blum, but he appreciated the sentiment. "Thank you, Popcorn. That's … very helpful."

"You bet, big guy," Popcorn said. "If you need me, I just need to do my inhaler before I get too much more excitement."

Lathrop said, "I'm duly chastened. Now, Mister Russell—"

YEARRRRRRRRRRRRRRRRRRRRRRRRRGH

An unholy roar blasted them from outside the four wasp-body walls of their tiny fort, making everyone sitting inside slam themselves flat against a wasp or double over into a defensive position. Then a furry pentadactyl paw the size of a car tire and the color of street slush swooped in and grabbed Natasha the Organization operative, swiping her out of the encampment and out of sight.

Lathrop moved to rise, but Brett held him down and yell-whispered, "*No!* You don't know how many there are! Stay down, for God's sake!"

"She is *vital!*"

"How?" Brett said, but then shook the thought out of his head and said, "We can't risk losing anybody else. I don't know what the hell that paw belongs to, but it has to be *huge*. It's way too dangerous to even stick your head out—"

"Crane!" Lathrop shouted in what was definitely not a whisper, "You and your men get your asses over the side and get her back! She is *vital!*"

Brett turned and looked at Crane, who was frozen between wanting to obey orders from his employer and really not wanting to get his head taken off by whatever hairy monster just ran off with a woman he didn't really talk to even once. Crane looked at his men, each of whom looked back with absolutely no hint of volunteering for the suicide mission of going after Natasha.

"You cowardly *bastards!* You'll be lucky if I pay a single one of you!"

Each commando—including Crane—had a submachine gun across his lap. At Lathrop's angry words, the muzzles all subtly, but unmistakably, were shifted to point right at him.

"I'm being hyperbolic, of course," Lathrop said lightly, but quickly regained his serious tone: "But we need her back! She is—"

"Vital?" Brett snarked, but quickly regained *his* serious tone: "No one except me and you is irreplaceable on this expedition, pal."

All through the sight of seeing Brett wrestling a crocodile and an anaconda, almost going down with a ship being attacked by a sea monster, and running from ginormous wasps and megapedes, Lathrop had never seemed more than a bit ruffled. But the way he now spoke showed that the Russian woman probably not named Natasha was probably a lot more *vital* than Brett believed even ten seconds earlier. Lathrop said in an almost-panicked voice, "*No!*

Mister Russell, you don't understand—Natasha is the reason we're *here*."

"Wait—her name really is Natasha?"

"What? No, her name is none of your business. But that woman had better still be alive and you all had better go retrieve her or *there is no expedition.*"

"Lathrop, *there is no expedition* if we're all dead! I'm sorry, but there's no way in hell any of us should risk our own lives to rescue any one member of the—"

RRRRREAAAARRRRRRRRRRRRRRRRRRRRRGH

The new roar was followed by the appearance of another hairy hand, which also reached over the top of the wasp's bodies—and grabbed Ellie. This time, however, the thing attached to the giant paw didn't remain low to the ground, which it and its compatriot must have done in order to sneak up on the makeshift fort.

It stood now, Ellie screaming from within its clutches like Fay Wray. Her scream came from at least thirty feet up, and the top of the thing's head was at least ten feet higher than that. It swept its great hairy leg over the top of the encampment and started walking away.

To the south. Every remaining person within the wasp fort put their head over the top and watched the impossibly tall and impossibly ugly orange ape-monster walk in the opposite direction from the one they wanted to go. In the distance ahead of this one strode the one that snatched Natasha. Its fist was still closed like the others' fingers were closed around the screaming Ellie White, so maybe the *vital* woman was still alive as well.

After a moment, every head turned to Brett, whose face still registered only shock. A few seconds went by before he came to his senses and shouted, "We have to go after them!"

If Lathrop had anything to say about the sudden change in his expedition leader's attitude toward rescuing any group members abducted by monsters, he kept it to himself. Brett could see the amusement on the commandos' faces, and he supposed he deserved a little ribbing, if not outright derision; he could take it, if it meant they would go along with getting Ellie back.

"What were those things that stole *TMI* host Ellie White?" Ravi asked Brett, with Stefan was on the job holding the camera at him.

"Guys, not right now—"

"Ellie would want us to be doing this, Mister Russell," Stefan said.

And he was right. She was an amazing woman, and it's just what she would want. Brett thought with an inward smile that what she'd probably *really* want right then was for him to stop screwing around with Sam and Dean over her and come to her rescue already. But he had a second to say, "Ithaqua, the Wind-Walker. You might know it as the Wendigo."

"*What?* For real?"

"For real. Now get that camera out of my face, okay? I gotta go save your boss."

Ravi said defensively, "She's not my boss. I'm *her* boss."

"Well, great job, boss—you put your employee in danger. If she gets hurt or killed, guess what? When we get back to the surface, OSHA's gonna come for your ass."

"I mean, I—"

"But don't worry about that, because I will already have killed you with my bare hands," Brett said.

Then he felt a hand on his shoulder again. "And he won't be alo—"

"Shut up, Popcorn."

~~~

There was no more argument; they were going after the Ithaqua, which had to be the most cryptid of any Brett had hunted so far. It was practically mythical, not to one culture but to all, even though it was usually known as the Wendigo outside of the writings of H.P. Lovecraft. Of course, Brett didn't know if this was what the ancient legends were referring to—Wendigos ate human flesh and stripped away souls and all of that, but Lovecraft's version simply stalked off with its victims later to drop them from a great height. Brett enjoyed the senseless evil of Lovecraft's monsters, and this was surely the purest pointlessly nasty creature in any of his work. Ithaqua didn't do anything to its victims except kill them by letting them fall from hundreds of feet (Lovecraft's Wendigo was impossibly tall; the thing they just saw must have stretched the outer limits of the cube-square rule limiting the size of terrestrial creatures and was probably one-tenth the height of Ithaqua.)

As if he could read Brett's mind—something that kind of surprised Brett, since he didn't feel confident the man could read at all—Crane asked point blank, "What the hell *are* those things?"

Brett didn't get a chance to answer him, as Ravi rushed to share his own cryptid expertise with the group as they gathered themselves and their things to go after the monsters, Natasha, and Ellie: "They're *wendigos*, Commander. The word comes from the Algonquin word *wiindigoo*, of course. They're described in myths shared by everyone from the Ojibwe to the Naskapi as cannibalistic monsters or manifestations of an evil spirit, or both. They have aspects of humanity, but aren't human, obviously, despite their walking upright and possession of hands with four fingers and an opposable thumb, so I suppose the term 'cannibalistic' isn't strictly accurate. They also are known to be shapeshifters, but that might not be completely accurate."

"*That* might not?" Popcorn echoed incredulously. "The whole thing is impossible."

Brett smirked. "This coming from a man who fought the world's largest dinosaur predator and now just watched a forty-foot ape-man kidnap two people."

"Well, perhaps not *impossible*. But darn it, it's still all pretty unbelievable." He paused, looking over the four paramilitary mercenaries, the crocodile wrestler, and the operative of a murderous global cabal, and added, "Please excuse my language."

Ravi went on: "There is a similar overtly mythical creature called the Wechuge, which is detailed through the oral tradition of the Athabaska from the Northwest Pacific. In any case, these creatures may seem humanlike in another aspect separate from their appearance: I'm thinking that perhaps they cook their food. That would explain why they took off with the agent and our show's host."

And the only person I've ever loved except my murdered wife and son. "Whatever it is, we have to travel *south* now, away from the mountains that are the most likely place for Merco to hide out. We need to get our people back. Apparently, Natasha is *vital*, and I can tell you Ellie is a lot more than that." He took a deep breath. "Let's go get them back. No monsters are going to steal our women and get away with it!"

They all shared a much-needed laugh and rose together to strike back—

"*God in Heaven!*" Stefan shouted, almost dropping the camera as something new came into the frame. Several things. And they looked hungry.

"What in hell are *those?*" Lathrop spouted. "Jackals? Hyenas?"

"Not unless jackals and hyenas have six legs," Brett said, but they did look a lot like the scavengers. But these were *long*, and an extra pair of legs supported them in the middle. Their mouths and the fangs within them were huge and dripping with drool no doubt triggered by a sudden big meal laid out right in front of them. He looked around them and counted off the creatures. "Six of them. There's nine of us. Any suggestions?"

"Stay here until they go away," Popcorn said flatly.

"That's not gonna save anybody."

Popcorn didn't have to say the words, since his sentiment was right there on his face: *I'm okay with that.* It was not, perhaps, his finest hour. But he made up for it: "Then let's go, right? Let's get away from them and save our women!" He paused. "Not to be sexist. But they *are* both women, technically speaking."

"Wow, okay, Popcorn is on board," Brett said with a look at the rest of them that was both a shaming and a dare. "Commandos, each of you take one side and just shoot any damn thing that doesn't look friendly."

"You don't order my men around, Russell."

Brett put his palms up in a "no offense" gesture. "Sorry."

Crane nodded at the apology and addressed his men: "Let's do what he said."

"Good work, Commander." Brett watched the jackal-things slowly circling the fort but not coming any nearer. "Now, we need to get out of here and … and, um …"

His words trailed off as he saw one of the animals sniff at the edge of the wasp carcass that was outside the four making up their encampment, because it recoiled and backed away. Considering that all of the creatures' legs and flanks were thick with horizontal lines of scar tissue, no doubt from a lifetime of rubbing up against the leaves of acid-plants, the jackal-things didn't shy away from anything easily.

The plants wouldn't touch the wasp bodies, either. He didn't know what it was about the steel-gray super-insects that repelled things down there, but he knew a possible advantage when he saw one. "Guys, those things out there won't get near these wasps. They want us really bad, but they want to avoid the wasp bodies even more."

"Superior," Lathrop said. "Now we may starve to death inside our little fort in peace."

"Nice attitude. People, listen to what I'm saying: maybe there's something with the wasps we can use, something to keep the jackal-things away from us long enough that we can get to wherever the wendigos are taking Ellie. And Natasha."

"We can't shoot 'em?" Flattop asked, looking genuinely crestfallen.

"No, you can—" Brett started to say, but *POP! POP! POP! POP! POP!* the commandos dropped every one of them in less than three seconds. "Okay, then! Good shootin', fellas!"

"I believe I understand where you're going with this, Mister Russell," Popcorn said. "We need to carve out these wasp corpses and travel within them as we go after the wendigos, right? It looks like each could fit two to three people within it. We could slice one open, pull out the ichor and spiracles and glands and guts and such, then carve some arm and leg holes, maybe take off the face in front so we can see … it could work! I mean, we're all wearing boots and long dungarees, so any really low plants that brush up against us won't get through, not for a long time, anyway."

"That's so disgusting, it might just work," Ravi said, and everyone shared a laugh. After a moment, he added, "No, but I really do think that will work."

Brett nodded and said to Lathrop, "You're just gonna have to throw that suit *out* when you get back, all the bug goo that'll be on it."

"Alas, yes. It's especially sad, since it cost more than you make in a year."

"I don't know, crocodile wrestling in a tiny rainforest village pays pretty well," he said, and laughed. "But yeah, that suit costing you so much is what makes it getting ruined so awesome."

~~~

They managed to drag the outside wasp carcass next to the walled-off area, making damned sure that the huge stinger didn't touch anyone. It wouldn't do to split it open and pour out its guts inside their one relatively safe place, and it definitely wouldn't do to make it through all of this crap just to get stung to death by a dead wasp.

No more jackal-things had come close, but Leavitt the commando reported that he could see several circling at about a one-hundred-yard perimeter, looking toward them the whole time. The hope was that whatever it was about the wasps that pushed all the various killer things away—even the wendigo didn't actually touch them—would hold at least as long as it took them to get to the southern reach, maybe even the northern mountains.

It was hard to judge distance in this alien environment, but the mountains looked to be a two hours' walk away; the wendigos were still much closer, but each step they took was like five human steps. Unless the giants stopped soon, they would quickly be farther from them than the mountains. And Brett had to get Ellie back.

Not just back to the group. He needed to *get Ellie back.* He would get the information, she and her crew would get the money, and they could be together. The Organization would have to give up on him now that he would have the goods on them, for fear that he might have set up a public airing of the information should something *unexpected* happen to him.

He knew he could get her back. But first, he had to literally get her back.

Crane used his machete to cut a seam down the middle of the bottom of the wasp's thorax, then let the thing fall onto its side and let its innards spill out onto the ground. Brett was curious as to whether any of the plants on the edge of their little clearing would like what was inside of one of the mega-wasps, even though they didn't care for their outer shell.

But it was like they had poured lye on the ground instead of the wasp's guts: the moment they touched any of the plant stems, the plants curled up, dried out, and turned black.

On the "Do acid-plants like wasp ichor?" question, then, Brett marked this down as a "no."

"That is some effective evolutionary adaptation," Popcorn said—then puked hard as the stench hit him. He wasn't the only one, either; in fact, the only people who didn't throw up were Brett, Lathrop, and Crane. And even they gagged.

"I just want to say that I am having *such* a pleasant adventure," Ravi said, wiping his mouth on his shirtsleeve.

"If you like that smell now," Brett said, "you'll *love* it when our heads are inside."

More puking.

Brett laughed, but he was pretty sure he'd be hurling like everybody else as soon as he had to breathe that in. However, he learned in the rich aromatic environment of tropical rainforests from Africa to South America that it takes only about five minutes to get so used to a smell that you don't even notice it any longer. One had to avoid getting away from and re-encountering the odor in question, but the constant up-close exposure each of them would have inside the carcass looking out should keep them from becoming completely dehydrated from vomiting. Brett had yet to see a water source down there, and the bottles of water in the commandos' bags wouldn't last very long.

As they worked to cut the cartilage and whatever the hell else kept the giant wasps in the shape of giant wasps, Brett realized that he had absolutely no sense of how long they had been in this weird world within the world. They hadn't stopped since they got there, first with the plants and then the wasps and the megapedes and the wendigo and now the six-legged jackals that, Brett noticed as he let some of the others spell him on the carving out the giant bug and stared out at the area around them, had made the radius of their circle much smaller in just a few minutes. Wasn't the smell bothering them, or could they have gotten used to it as well?

Had they been there for two hours, or eight? Or even ten? There had been an enormous amount of trudging through the sizzling acid-plants, and fighting the various creatures had taken much longer in reality than it seemed to in Brett's mental reconstructions. There was no sun and no clouds. His watch, like anything electronic, didn't seem to work down under the island. Maybe it was a good thing they weren't dragging that high-end arsenal that depended on computers and electronic components even to start up, let alone aim or fire.

The place was a mystery. It seemed like a dream. A nightmare, but a damned weird one, that was for sure. At least in dreams, none of them could—

"Gah! *Aieeeeeeee!*"

Brett had no idea what triggered it, but faster than Brett could react in his pensive state, one of the jackal-things made a direct run at the encampment and clamped its big jaws around the ankle of Todd the commando. The man screamed as his leg was pulled out from under him, he went down hard onto the ground, and was ripped away from them by the unbelievably fast cryptid, which sprinted away to the east. After a few seconds, they couldn't hear Todd's screams anymore, maybe because he was out of earshot, maybe because he was unconscious, maybe because he was dead.

None of the other jackal-things followed the attacker. But they did move closer.

Flattop was pale as a sheet at what had just happened to his comrade. "You sons of bitches!" he yelled at the top of his lungs, and he moved to bring up his AK-47 and end the lives of every last one of the creatures.

But Crane smacked his hand down on the rifle and kept Flattop from lifting it at the animals. "That'll attract more, soldier. Stand down."

For all his idiocy, Brett saw, Crane could be an effective commander. Brett hadn't considered that the new pack of jackal-things was attracted by the gunfire that rang out when the first pack was shot down. He didn't know what to do, and that bothered him since it happened to him so rarely in the field. On the one hand, it would be nice to have these suckers dead so they could get all the wasps carved out and get moving after the wendigos; but on the other, if they sound would attract even more, they'd be screwed thanks to the reduced speed and ability to see once the wasp husks were over their heads. They weren't quick enough to get away from the lightning-fast creatures anyway, but at least they could try to have some kind of maneuverability. But in the hard shells looking only forward and the fact that they would need to coordinate their steps like they were in a two-person horse costume at a party meant that they would be completely at the mercy of the hungry cryptids. And they didn't look like things that would show prey much mercy.

"So we're gonna wear these things like a canoe over our heads?" Crane asked, scraping out the last of the goo from inside the first dead wasp.

"That's the plan." Brett picked up one of the commandos' machetes and had the men position the wasp so its horrible face was accessible. Then he raised the machete and chopped right behind the creepy giant compound eyes. It went a third of the way through. Brett had to swing the big blade three more times to get it most of the way off, then sawed through the last bit of chitinous exoskeleton. The face came off and sank onto the dirt.

"This is easily the most revolting thing I've ever experienced," Lathrop said. He remained sitting inside the compound, where he had quickly retreated when the jackal-things carried off Todd the commando. He patted his brow with a handkerchief, although Brett had no idea why the Organization man, who had done nothing with the wasp or anything else, would be perspiring.

"Just wait 'til you get inside," Brett said with a laugh, then addressed everyone: "All right, guys, this is how this is going to work. You see that we have the shell of this thing, like the commander said, it's like a overturned canoe. There are eight of us, and I think two people per shell would be a good compromise between mobility and efficiency. Each set of two will get under and inside the shell, and … Crane, would you help me demonstrate?"

Crane stepped up and helped Brett pick up the hollowed-out wasp and lift it over their heads and down. The three-foot-deep carcass left most of their legs unprotected. Brett said loudly from inside the thing so everyone could hear, "If you come under attack, just crouch down, like this." He and Crane bent their knees and crouched, which brought the wasp down to where the only part of their bodies visible were their feet in boots. "The plants won't be able to get us as we walk by, and it seems like the other creatures really don't like whatever these wasps are giving off. We can make good time by walking in step."

"What about holes for guns?" That was Flattop.

"Or cameras?" That was Stefan.

Brett hadn't considered that, but improvised as best he could: "If you want to keep your weapon—or camera—at hand, you'll have to be in the front of the wasp and point it out the face-hole."

Flattop looked fine with that; Stefan less so, but he was a trouper. "All for the glory of *TMI*."

"I'll drink to that," Ravi said, and drained the last of the water that Crane had given him. "I will also drink any water he happens to come across. How can plants and animals live with no water?"

"I doubt they have *no* water," Popcorn sniffed. "These plants and animals all seem to employ cellular structure and function exactly as their analogs in the world above. I would think that the vegetation accesses water underground—even this underground world has an underground, it can be safely assumed—and the animals and insects get it from some pools at the surface or just by eating one another."

Ravi stared. "Thanks, I feel *so* much better now."

"You are most welcome. Knowledge is power, after all!"

Brett was still smiling at that when he and Crane lifted the heavy wasp shell off them and placed it back on the ground. "We need to get the rest of these carved out fast and get moving if we're going to catch those things that stole Ellie and Natasha."

"For God's sake, can we please stop calling her 'Natasha'?" Lathrop whined.

"Sure! What's her real name, then?"

"I don't know, but I highly doubt it is 'Natasha' just because she has a Russian accent."

Brett meant it when he said, "How can you not know this woman's name? Who *is* she anyway? She's not with the

Organization, or else you'd know her. Or she'd just be in charge here instead of you."

"As I told you and everyone else, Mister Russell, she is the vital element we need if this whole misadventure is going to produce the results that I and my employer seek. You truly have no need for any other information about this woman."

Brett thought for a moment and looked at Lathrop with narrowed eyes and an amused expression. "You don't *know* who she is, do you? I don't just mean her name—I mean the Organization is keeping you in the dark. You only know that your head is on the chopping block if we can't retrieve the good doctor, and she is somehow *vital* to doing that. Correct?"

Lathrop sighed and said, "Indeed, you are correct, Mister Russell. Are you happy now? Can we please get this whole circus caravan moving now?"

"All right," Brett said with great amusement and proceeded to prepare three more wasp carcasses for their pursuit and rescue mission-within-a-mission. Once those were done, the group split into four duos, the first in front and the second in back: Brett with Lathrop, Stefan (because of the camera) with Crane, Flattop with Ravi, and Leavitt with Popcorn.

"I don't see the wendigos anymore," Brett said, making sure the wasp's face-hole was turned so the others could hear him; once they were all pointing in the same direction, it would be very hard to hear anyone else not inside the same shell. "Maybe they're lying down and resting, or maybe they just walked too far and are obscured by trees. Either way, we're going after them—no Natasha, who I'm totally going to keep calling 'Natasha,' no mission. And Ellie because she's *Ellie*, dammit."

"Right on," Ravi said in a muffled bit of support.

"Let's move out."

They formed a single line, even though going side by side may have been a better choice in different circumstances. But going in single file, everyone could see if they were going in the same direction and at the same speed: Brett's wasp in front, followed by Stefan's, then Flattop, and finally Crane at the rear so he could spin around and shoot behind the line, if that became necessary.

Brett was bothered that he could no longer see the wendigos. It wasn't exactly worry, because he'd found long before that worrying didn't produce good results. Being bothered, annoyed, even outraged were all effective motivational emotions in Brett's experience, whereas being worried was rarely about anything other than itself. But damn, he was seriously bothered, especially since he had once again lost track of time while they were working on the wasp carcasses. They had all been thirsty, and thank God the commandos brought a good amount of extra water, although it wasn't really "extra," since they carried it to drink themselves. However, although they were guns for hire, they didn't seem to be bad people: they wanted everyone to make it. Brett found that highly commendable ... and hoped no more of them got eaten in the line of duty.

They marched for what felt like an hour, all of them sweating profusely. It warmed Brett's heart to think of Lathrop right behind him getting dirty and sweaty and hopefully humiliated as they walked, but he also hoped Popcorn wasn't going to throw up, pass out, or die from how hot it was inside the shells. So far, there had been no complaints, at least none that he could hear from the front of the line.

That changed, however, as they entered an area more dense with trees that any they had walked through down there before. Even just looking straight ahead in order to find the best path through the acid-dripping foliage, Brett could see shapes between the trees and could hear heavy footfalls. There were *things* in this copse, big things. Although they were protected as far as they knew within their wasp shells, they also knew that new dangers abounded in this hostile land.

But that was all a distraction, because at the exit from the wooded area stood three of the jackal-things, slavering with anticipation at the sight of prey moving through their hunting ground. Brett yelled as loud as he could, "*Halt!*" No one ran into him, so he assumed the wasp team directly behind him heard, and he could hear Stefan yell "*Halt!*" and then Flattop in the wasp behind Stefan follow suit.

Brett led Lathrop in turning their wasp around so he could address the others, who formed a semi-circle around him as he spoke. "You guys see the jackals ahead? They're standing between us and the treeless space we need to get across."

"Great," Brett could hear Ravi mutter.

"Yeah, I agree it's non-optimal. But here we are. I think the wasp bodies will keep them from attacking us directly, but they could try to knock us over and then drag us away by our feet like poor Todd."

"If I had any water left, I'd pour some of it out for our dead homie," Crane said, completely without irony.

"Um, yeah, of course," Brett said. "We all would. But what I'm saying is that we may get through them okay, but we may not and then we would be killed and eaten by six-legged dog-monsters."

"What are our options, Mister Russell?" That was Lathrop right behind him.

The Organization man spoke inconsiderately quietly, so Brett was forced to repeat Lathrop's question for the rest before he said, "I don't really know if we *have* any options. If anyone has any suggestions …"

Brett could hear Popcorn's voice and almost smiled as he imagined him trying to politely raise his hand inside the wasp carcass over his head: "Couldn't we just wait them out, see if they get discouraged and go away?"

"The wendigos will be too far off then," Lathrop said. "We must act swiftly."

"As distasteful as I find it, I agree with him on this. But I can't decide for the group. I mean, I *can*, and maybe I *should*, but this could be a suicide run even if it's the only way to get to Ellie. And Natasha. So let's take a vote. As the head of this expedition, I reserve the right—"

"*I'm* the head of this expedition, Mister Russell."

Brett sighed. "As the *leader* of this expedition, I reserve the right to veto the decision, but I need to know where my people are on this. All in favor of rushing the jackal-things, say 'aye'—"

"*Aieeeeeeeeeeeeeeeeeeee!*" came a scream from Popcorn as his and Leavitt's wasp shell was knocked sideways and then thrown to the ground by a truck-sized bird that must have been perched on a high branch. Its skin shone gray and scaly—it wasn't a bird.

It was a goddamn *pterodactyl*.

The dinosaur reached down with its long beak and stabbed up into wasp shell, running Leavitt right through the center of his body and sliding him out like a piece of shrimp plucked out of a Chinese takeout carton. Leavitt was already dead by the time the pterodactyl raised his body up and shook it hard, spraying all the other wasp carcasses with the commando's blood and organs. Then it whipped the body into the air and caught it to slide right down its gullet like a waterfowl gulping down a tasty fish.

An AK-47 poked out the front of Flattop and Ravi's wasp and blasted out shot after shot at the beast, but the bullets barely seemed to register more than making the twenty-foot-tall lizard-bird twitch a little. Undaunted, it swept back down to pull Popcorn from the overturned wasp body, but before it could get to him, a Coke-sized black can flew toward the thing's head in a long arc, almost as if whoever threw it was trying to have it take a few extra seconds.

Which is how Crane meant to throw the concussion grenade. It came down at the back of the pterodactyl's head just at the moment it exploded, neatly separating the creature's skull from its spine. Its brain and body no longer being connected, the dinosaur wobbled and then fell to the ground with its tons of weight, missing Popcorn still prone inside the wasp shell by less than two feet.

The rest of them cheered. It was a brilliant move on Crane's part, Brett thought, once again seeing that book-knowledge and field-knowledge were not one and the same: with a regular grenade, Popcorn or any of them might have been hit with flying shrapnel. But by using the concussion grenade and timing it perfectly, Crane could kill the monster without endangering anyone else.

"Well done," Brett said, but even he didn't know how well-done it was until he saw rashes of creatures, things that looked like nightmare versions of six- and eight-legged animals from the size of cats to the size of horses descend from the trees and immediately start feeding on the still-warm carrion that less than a minute earlier was going to kill every last human on the expedition. The dozen—*dozens*—of creatures that set upon the dead pterodactyl completely ignored Brett and his contingent … but that wouldn't last.

And the jackal-things hadn't budged from the middle of their only path out of the woods.

Popcorn had pulled himself out of his and the late Leavitt's wasp husk and brushed some of the ichor and bits of cartilage from his red sweater. He looked at the feeding frenzy not ten feet away, then cast his gaze to the high treetops. "I'd venture that the tops of the trees aren't acidic. There's probably not going to be enough prey up there to make it worth the evolutionary expense, since anything they started to eat up there would just climb down or fall down onto the dirt, where that particular tree wouldn't be able to get to them. So, perhaps, this strange bestiary simply waits up there until something tasty walks by."

Despite all of his time battling dangerous cryptids in woods, rainforests, and deserts, Brett had to suppress a shudder. *They* might have been that something tasty if the dinosaur hadn't shown up.

"And Commander Crane, thank you for coming to my aid."

"Don't mention it," Crane said, already staring at the jackal-things and no doubt wondering how he could take them out as well. "Now we got to get out of this place and get the giants that stole our women."

"Working on it," Brett said, then addressed Popcorn: "Do you think you can manage that wasp shell on your own? We can't afford to leave one behind, since we'll need it when we bring Ellie back. And Natasha."

Popcorn looked at the heavy canoe-like wasp body dubiously. "I doubt it."

"Yeah, I can see that." Everyone had laid their wasp shells down and were having a bit of fresh air since they were just standing there anyway. There were Brett and Lathrop, Stefan and Crane, Flattop and Ravi, and now Popcorn without the unfortunate Leavitt. "We don't have enough commandos to go around now, though. What if we put Ravi with Stefan, and then Popcorn can go with Flattop? We'll put Ravi and Stefan in the middle so they're protected even though they don't have a soldier with them. Okay, Crane, can you take Lathrop off my hands? I can manage the bug canoe by myself long enough to get to the wendigos—we're going to need all four protective carcasses once we get our people back."

Crane could and did. Everyone moved to their respective bugs, Brett by himself in front, then Stefan with Ravi, Popcorn with Flattop, and finally Crane with Lathrop. The Organization man didn't care for being at the more vulnerable end of the line, but Brett wasn't overly concerned with what Lathrop wanted at this point. Crane was obviously a superior soldier; Brett didn't think Lathrop was in any more danger, and possibly less, than any of the rest of them.

Regardless of how much danger the man was or wasn't in, however, he was still a huge pain in the ass. "What is the *plan* here, Mister Russell? Do you even have a plan, other than for us to don these disgusting corpses again and try to just run past the killer dingoes?"

Brett thought for a moment, smiled, and said, "No, that's pretty much the plan. If you have anything better in mind, please don't hold back. We want to hear it."

"Oh, of *course* I don't have anything better in mind, you musclebound circus freak. Let's get on with it," Lathrop snarled, and motioned for Crane to get the damned thing over their heads already.

Somebody's getting testy, Brett thought with amusement. For all he knew, Lathrop could give him information that was false; in fact, with the Organization, that was likely to be true. But seeing Lathrop having a really unpleasant time was a lot of payment in itself. He had taken the job thinking Lathrop was legit, but of course he knew there was always the possibility he was still working for the Organization, which turned out to be the case.

All of that being said, however, there were two reasons why Brett still believed that, should he make it out of this found world alive and having retrieved this Doctor Merco, he would indeed be receiving accurate information about the murder of his family: First, surely even someone as full of himself as Lathrop knew that, since Brett knew his identity (even if the name was fake), Lathrop would definitely die by his hand should he give Brett a false lead. Brett would find him again and kill him tortuously slowly. But the second factor was even more prevalent in Brett's mind, and that was that the soulless executives of the Organization would sell one of their own out in a nanosecond if it meant that they would profit from the betrayal. It wasn't hard to imagine the Organization exec who ordered Brett's wife and child to be killed in order to keep Brett focused on his work getting sold out by a different exec who wanted to score points with the higher-ups by bringing this renegade scientist and his superweapon back home. What did that second evil S.O.B. care if Brett would almost certainly kill the first evil S.O.B.? The answer was *not at all*. The very nature of the Organization was power over all. If that meant one member of the C-Suite was fatally exposed by another seeking greater power, then that was practically fulfilling the mission statement.

Brett shook his head. He'd be scared to see what the Organization's "mission statement" even looked like. Did they have one? Was there also a mission statement in hell?

He had to shake himself out of his metaphysical reverie. Before he got the dead wasp on his shoulders again, he said to the group, "We're going to just plow forward as fast as we can move. I don't know how the jackal-things will react, but I'm pretty sure we don't want to stay around while more scavengers come for the big meal we just laid out for them. Those of you with weapons"—he hefted Leavitt's AK-47—"shoot anything that gets too near. *Let's go!*"

With that, Brett threw himself into the wasp shell, got it balanced, and started marching forward as fast as his legs would take him as he bore the weight of his bug-canoe alone. They all had to just keep walking and not look behind them, from where the squelching and sucking sounds of scores of sharp-toothed scavengers tore open the pterodactyl and started feeding. What was harder than not looking back was not trying to run to get away from the horrors. This was tempered, however, by the sight of the hungry jackal-things getting excited as they watched their prey coming to *them*. Every one of the cryptids hunkered down now, ready to jump onto them even though they could see nothing but four giant wasps walking toward them. Did they smell all that different? Was it smell that made the jackal-things back off in the first place? If so, then maybe they could keep them at enough of a distance and walk past and away from them quickly enough that the creatures wouldn't have a chance to get used to the smell.

Brett realized that he really didn't know much of anything. He had the tracking and adventuring capabilities for this mission, of course, but he lacked any advance knowledge about the cryptids they were encountering—other than the wendigo, which was in his more familiar "cultural myth" category of monster he often hunted. The rest, though ... six-legged canines? Acid-plants? Giant bugs? Thank God there was a good old pterodactyl! Dinosaurs were at least a monster he knew; in fact, he wished they had dinosaurs in front of them instead of these monsters literally salivating at the sight of them.

As he reached the edge of the wooded area and was just ten feet from the biggest jackal-thing, a gigantic shape darkened the sky: twenty feet high, thirty feet long, with jaws supporting three-foot-long pointed teeth and a small crest at the top of its head and walking on two massive reptilian legs: *Allosaurus*.

Why can't I keep my big mouth shut? Brett wondered as he fell to the side to avoid running right into the *Allosaurus*'s path, which was from the side, going straight toward the jackal-things—

"*Jesus!*"

—and gobbling up and crushing the biggest one in its mouth.

Brett slammed on the brakes, and the shell behind him ran into him and knocked him into the dirt. Then the one behind that crashed into it, and the fourth into the third. All of them were on the ground now, looking up at the spectacle: the magnificent allosaur used its massive jaws to toss the broken jackal-thing into the air. It arced back down right into the dinosaur's mouth and was swallowed whole.

Another allosaur appeared, and between them, they ate four of the six-legged cryptids and shook the rest until their spines broke and left their dead bodies on the ground.

Great, they hunt for fun. Brett didn't see any way around them, and now the two allosaurs—what was it with lost worlds and frickin' dinosaurs, anyway?—milled about in front of their egress point from the acid-woods, just kind of walking back and forth. Every now and then one of them would look toward the humans and their wasp shells, but then just looked away again. After a while, everyone stood up and took off their protective wasp bodies to wait out the giant lizards.

"I've seen enough *Jurassic Park* to know that they can't see us if we're not moving," Crane said. "All we need to do is figure out a way to get past them without moving."

Everyone stared at him.

"I, uh … I guess that would be kinda hard," he added, and then shut up.

Brett cleared his throat and said to everyone, "All right, here's the situation: we have two very hungry *dinosaurs* waiting for us at the only exit we've seen to get out of this thicket of woods. Every minute we're here, the wendigos take Ellie—and Natasha—that much farther away. We may be clear of the jackal-things for the moment, but God knows what else is out there even if we can get past these two monsters. Any suggestions?"

"There must be another path out of here," Lathrop said. "We can just walk through the plants a bit more—as you said, we do have clothing on to protect us the little ways we have to walk to get out. All of you, even the *television people*, have boots on, while I have only my Salvatore Ferragamos, and those have been entirely ruined. If *I* am the one suggested we find another way out, certainly that must mean something given the personal and property risk that doing so involves."

Everyone stared at Lathrop now.

"You may take your expressions of scorn and put them up your backsides. Mister Russell, I demand a vote. Ayes support finding a different way out; nays insist on staying here and waiting until the dinosaurs get tired or some such. May we vote?"

"Why, sure," Brett said. "Who wants to rustle around in the acid garden here and let the various monsters eating the pterodactyl come after us when they're done? Or, on the other side, who wants to stay here and let the various monsters eating the pterodactyl come after us when they're done?"

"That seems like a bit of biased phrasing, but yes."

"Fine. All those who—"

"Wait," Popcorn interrupted, "isn't there a third option? Such as just going for it and running past them inside our protective wasp remains?"

Ravi spoke up: "Did you see what they did to those monster dingoes or whatever they are? They moved like lightning. We wouldn't stand a chance."

Brett cast an eye at the things digging into the dead pterodactyl; the flying dinosaur didn't have a lot of meat on it compared to other prehistoric beasts, and the scavengers would be done soon. The allosaurs killed just to kill, and there was no guarantee even these full monsters wouldn't rip every one of the humans apart before the commandos could get their guns raised.

Stefan took the camera from his eye for a moment. "Maybe the wasp shells will turn off the dinosaurs like they did the dingoes."

Brett wanted to say, *They're jackal-things, not dingo-things. I already named them, thank you very much.* But instead he said, "Look, I'm glad we can have some open dialogue about this, but we need to decide what exactly we're going to do. So, we can try to find another way out, even though that means giving those bastards over there a chance to kill us; or we can just try to wait out the dinosaurs, with the same effect; or we can try to run past them wearing our wasps and hoping it repels the allosaurs."

"Yeah, but the shells could slow us down too much," Flattop said. "I say we just run for it without the shells. All we gotta do is stay really near their feet—that way their maneuverability is gonna be all compromised."

These commandos were idiotic until it came to battle strategy, Brett noticed again. The *Spinosaurus* he had fought was four-legged but alone. These dinosaurs were bipedal, which would make it a little bit safer because they would need to pivot in place and thus not sweep their legs in an effort to turn like a quadruped would. This meant that none of them would be likely to get kicked to death, but the upright beasts might be able to attack the other's foot area to get the tasty morsels hiding within. "That's excellent, soldier," Brett said. "We need to run as fast as we can carrying the supply bags right under the allosaurs and then keep running while they're confused."

"Why don't we just shoot them?" Ravi asked.

Popcorn answered, "We've already seen how noise attracts other unsavory predators. I think fighting one killer species at a time is difficult enough without inviting others to the party."

"Ah, yeah, right. Good point."

"So, we are to flee back out into the wild without any protection whatsoever?" Lathrop said as snottily as ever.

Brett said, "Unless you have a better idea." He nodded at the scavengers which, as he had expected, starting to cast glances their way as they finished up their meal. "And you'd better have it *fast*."

"All right, Mister Russell, have it your way. 'Once more unto the breach, dear friends, once more,' eh? Let us go and face our doom boldly."

"You're less Henry the Fifth and more Ass-clown the First."

"Witty, very witty, Mister Russell. Now … shall we?"

Brett smirked and had everyone collect whatever they had in preparation for making the run. "I don't have any plan for what happens once we get past these things—*if* we get past them. But I want everyone to run as close to the allosaurs' legs as possible. Step on a giant foot if you need to, just stick close where they can't bend down and pick you off. Ready? One … two …" As he turned away from them to lead them out, he saw something that chilled his blood: the scavenger monsters were abandoning the pterodactyl corpse and running straight toward them. "Oh my God—*follow me!*"

Some of the group looked around to see what had panicked their leader and saw the things coming after them. They shouted or screamed, depending on if it was Popcorn or not, and ran right behind Brett, who was heading for the feet of the dinosaur on their right. There wasn't any real reason he chose that one, but he had to choose one of them and that was it. He realized halfway between the edge of the woods and the feet of the *Allosaurus* that he should have sent some to the right and some to the left, since if they all went under only one, the other could go in and chomp them. *Too late now*, he thought, and reached the underside of the beast and kept on running. He could hear pounding feet behind him and knew at least some of them had made it through. He wasn't going to look back until he felt fairly sure that the dinosaurs weren't coming after them. If they *were* coming after him and his compatriots, Brett didn't see how they would escape—there was absolutely nothing ahead except low-lying plants as far as he could see. No protective copses or packs of things that would predate on one another, thus providing cover for their would-be meals to get the hell out of there.

When he felt like he had put a safe distance between himself and the dinosaurs, he allowed himself to turn his head as he ran to see if all of them made it. All of them had, with the exception of the struggling, overweight Popcorn—huffing and puffing at the end of the line, he just didn't move fast enough now that the allosaurs were alerted to the humans' presence. The one that had been on Brett's left just bent down like the pump above an oil well and closed his jaws around the screaming nerd. Then it straightened up and swallowed down the plumpest morsel that had tried to run by him.

Not Popcorn! Brett's mind yelled, but of course it was Popcorn. Now that it had happened, he realized, it had been in the cards from the beginning. And what made it more ironic was that he ended up being of no use to the mission at all once all the electronic equipment was lost in the sinking. He hoped that there wouldn't be too much technology to deal with once they got to the scientist, because Popcorn was their go-to guy on that. Brett didn't think there was much the good doctor could have made out of the materials around those parts, but if the Professor on *Gilligan's Island* could make a working radio out of coconuts and jungle vines, who knew what this guy could do.

All of that flew through his mind in the second before he turned his head back around to the front and kept running as fast as his powerful muscles could carry him. The others weren't far behind, but Ravi was definitely an indoor kid, and Stefan couldn't run very fast with the goddamn camera up to his face; but that was their problem for the moment. For Ellie, yes, he would have slowed down and tried to pull her along faster—but if Ellie was with them, *she* would probably be the one pulling *him*.

Ellie. After losing her for so long, he couldn't lose her again. Especially not like this. She was only there because of him, because Lathrop recruited her and brought her there as leverage or bait. Now, it seemed, she was both, since there was no way in hell he would be going south toward nothing instead of north toward—

"*Whoa! Stop! STOP!*" Brett shouted so loudly it hurt his throat. "There's a cliff! *THERE IS A CLIFF!*"

And there *was* a cliff. Without any warning whatsoever, the land dropped off at a 90-degree angle, to a perfect vertical. If Brett had been looking behind himself for five more seconds, he would have run right over the side. But his depth perception caught that part of what was in front of him was at least two hundred feet farther away. It was the far cliff wall. Beyond it was more of the exact type of landscape they had just been running through, rendering the chasm invisible until one was right up on it.

Everyone in the group was able to stop before they got to the edge. Brett was thankful that they had stayed in a single-file line instead of a horizontal *Chorus Line* rush, because some of them would definitely have fallen to their deaths. Or maybe just been horribly injured; he couldn't see how deep the chasm was until he carefully walked to the side, which he did now, peering down. Anybody falling off that cliff would definitely be dead … but that wasn't the worst thing about the definitely human-excavated cavity they almost had thrown themselves into.

"Holy …" Commander Crane muttered as he, too, got to the edge of the drop-off. "What the heck? The wendingos live here?"

Brett was too stunned to respond, whether to Crane or to any of the others who looked down into the chasm and saw the two forty-foot-tall Wind Walkers just standing inside the dug-out area that was still ten feet deeper than they were tall. The chasm itself was at least a football field across and stretched as far as they could see from their low vantage point. The very precision and smoothness of the cut boggled Brett's mind—how in the hell was that even possible? It didn't matter how it was possible, however; it was there and so were they and the wendigos as well. The two giant creatures passively stared up at the humans, looking no more demonic than a couple of orangutans blown up to incredible size in an Atomic Age horror movie.

There were the rudiments of giant proto-furniture at the bottom, humps that were flat at the top so they could be used as chairs or tables, he was sure of it. They hadn't found Doctor Merco yet, but this had to be his work. They had been forced to go the wrong way by the wendigos carrying Ellie and Natasha … but it had been the right way. There was evidence of the scientist's influence right in the front of them.

RARRRRRRRRRRRRRRRRRRR!

And right behind them, the two overexcited allosaurs. Brett had almost forgotten them in the ten seconds he had been staring down at the lair of the wendigos. He wasn't a scientist or anthropologist or even a cryptozoologist like his wife—still your ex-wife, pal, he had to remind himself—but the idea of cryptids possessing some human traits fascinated him. It made it more like they really were outside of science, but of course nothing was outside of science. Cryptids ceased to be cryptids once they were discovered and classified.

POW! POW! POW! POW! The commandos let loose against the two rushing dinosaurs, blasting them in a spray of high-caliber ballistics. Any worry that the prehistoric beasts wouldn't be affected by bullets disappeared immediately once the allosaurs started shrieking.

And Brett had thought their *roar* was loud! This was almost literally ear-splitting, forcing everyone to drop anything they were holding and slap their hands over their ears. The wendigos in the chasm covered their heads at the sound, too.

Although it seemed like forever, five seconds later the reptiles stopped shrieking and ran off to the east, hobbled a bit but otherwise seeming not too worse off for wear. Brett hated to see innocent creatures die, and the allosaurs and all of the deadly cryptids were just that: innocent. Humans had, once again, entered a pristine wilderness and started hacking away at any living thing that tried to defend its territory or even eat. He was glad to see the dinosaurs escape, but he wondered how long it would be until armies of humans started coming down the tunnels and overtaking this found world.

He looked down again at the wendigos placidly observing them from their place inside the pit. This must have been where they lived, since there was ample evidence of bones of all shapes and sizes down there with them. Were they fed by whoever built this pit? Or did they hunt? Or did animals just run right over the well-hidden cliff and literally fall into the giant monsters' hands? Probably a combination of all three.

"How do we get across?" Ravi asked, and the looks on the rest of the faces echoed his question. "I don't think we can go around. I can't even see where this ends."

Brett looked for any sign of a way across: something to climb down, even though that would mean they were in the skeleton-strewn pit with the Ithaqua. There were no trees he could see near the edge of the chasm, so using the grappling hooks wouldn't work. Maybe if they—

His line of thought was cut off by the sound of scraping metal coming from the far side of the chasm. He and everyone else watched in amazement as a five-foot-wide tongue of metal, slightly bowed in the middle, emerged from about twenty feet below the top of the cliff across from them. It slowly extended upward at an angle toward right where they were standing on the other side. It was a bridge across the chasm, and it was being extended specifically for them.

"This feels like a good sign and a bad sign at the same time," Flattop the commando said, sounding like he was just spilling the contents of his mind without necessarily meaning to. "A bridge, but, like, to *where*, y'know?"

But he was right. They were being welcomed, or at the very least allowed across. But why was the platform or drawbridge or whatever it was coming from a low angle and being stretched *up* to them?

His question was answered as a small door slid open in the cliff wall immediately above where the skinny metal stretch had emerged. It was five feet wide, like the platform, and five feet tall, making a perfect black square in the wall.

"It's not a bridge," Brett said. "It's a slide."

This conclusion was inescapable for everyone by the time the metal pathway reached the top lip of their side of the chasm wall and locked into place. They waited for any kind of instructions, maybe someone poking their head out of the door on the other side, but none came.

Brett kept his eye on the two wendigos, but the things seemed entirely uninterested in his group. Obviously they ate humans—some of those skeletons at the cryptids' feet were definitely *Homo sapiens sapiens.* He also noted that there were some ripped-apart Organization commando uniforms down there that exactly matched the ones that the two remaining soldiers of fortune, Crane and Flattop, were wearing. He hoped the men didn't notice this, because mercenaries could lose their nerve once their imminent death was duly pointed out to them. This was different from soldiers fighting for their country or from rebels fighting for some ideal: if you were dead, there was no money, and thus there was no point in risking your neck in the first place.

To this end, Brett said, "Down the slide first, boys—we need you to protect the front flank."

Crane and Flattop moved to obey, but Crane stopped and said to Brett, "Wait. Sorry, Mister Russell, but there's no such thing as a 'front flank.' What you got is sides that you call flanks—"

"Sorry, right, of course. What do you call the front line, then?"

"Um ... the front line is called 'the front line.'"

"Good to know. Now get down there and protect our front line!"

With the terminology settled, first Crane and then Flattop secured their supply bags to their chests, positioned themselves on the wide metal slide, crossed their arms across them and let gravity do the rest, pulling them down and across faster and faster until they whipped right into the black square opposite them and out of sight.

Then Brett sent Ravi, Stefan with his camera, and Lathrop; only then did he situate his butt on the slide, cross his arms, and zoom across the fifty-foot-deep man-made canyon into the darkness everyone else had disappeared into.

The landing area of the slide was well designed, as it used the angle and momentum of the entering body to allow the person to end up in a standing position. Brett laughed out loud at this and saw that everyone else in the small anteroom was smiling at this latest strange development in their adventure.

Brett took a moment to look around the perfectly cubical space inside which they now stood. Its proportions were roughly fifty feet by fifty feet by fifty feet, lighted by bioluminescence just as the "sky" was outside, but whatever chemical reaction was producing these photons, the light was as white and as bright as a fluorescent bulb. It made the perfection of the right angles defining the room starkly visible. For the first time in his entire career of hunting things denied by the scientific world, he wondered if he was observing the work of extraterrestrials. No human hand or even group of human hands could make something so perfectly smooth, especially not given the primitive conditions of this subterranean realm.

Everyone jumped as the sound of rock grinding against rock sounded throughout the chamber. They turned and saw a six-foot-high door open as part of the wall slid to the side. Out of the doorway stepped a plump sixty-something man with white hair and mustache with goatee, with his round metal glasses making him look a little like a chubby Sigmund Freud.

"That's him! That's Doctor Merco!" Lathrop shouted to the commandos. "Grab him! *Seize him!*"

There was no way that Lathrop didn't know he sounded exactly like a B-movie villain, Brett thought, and wanted so much to remind him how B movies usually turned out for the bad guy. But he didn't.

Instead, he stepped between the door where Doctor Merco was standing and the commandos, who had been so taken by surprise by Snidely Whiplash's order that they hadn't even fished their weapons out of the canvas bags they were stored in.

"Whoa, everybody just take a second here," Brett said calmly but forcefully, putting his hands up with palms forward to help stop the commandos from rushing forward. "Doctor Merco might have our only way out of here. I think it might be a bit premature to abduct him right off the bat."

Merco said in amusement, "So I'm getting abducted. I'd think some kidnappers would have found the element of surprise valuable in this situation, but what would I know? I'm apparently going to be the victim here."

Brett, hands still up in front of him in a so-far-effective position of *Hold on a minute*, turned to address the scientist: "Do you have Ellie White?"

"Yes, she said her husband would come for her, which I think is wonderful, both that she said it and that you did really did come. So romantic!" Merco said with sincerity, then smiled and somehow also frowned at the same time. "I'm really sorry about my silly wendigo grabbing the wrong person. They saw or maybe smelled two females in your group and so each one picked one of them up and brought them here. Or, at least, I assume that's what happened. Wendigos can be trained, but they can't speak to explain their thinking. They brought back two women, one of which was my target. Your wife is here, safe and sound—I couldn't very well toss her back out into that killer environment, especially not if her knight in shining armor was due any moment."

"Wait, how did you know we were out there in the first place? And that there was the woman you wanted with us? You couldn't possibly have cameras out there."

"No, not *cameras*—just one motion-activated radio-transmitting camera, posted where you exited the tunnel and entered Vulcania."

"Vulcania?" Ravi repeated. "Wait, I get it: the realm of the volcano."

"On the nose, sir! I built and installed it when the Organization goons destroyed the barricade I had built upon completing the tunnel."

"That must've been one big-ass door," Flattop said, and Lathrop slapped him in the arm to remind him what he was doing there, which was most certainly *not* to hold a friendly conversation with the target.

Merco smiled widely. "It wasn't a door, my friend. Doors are meant to be opened. The impenetrable barricade I constructed was meant to seal off the entrance forever." He thought for a moment and added, "Well, I suppose I shouldn't call it an *impenetrable* barricade anymore. Those mercenaries blew it up quite handily. In any case, the barrier was there not to keep humans out but to keep in Vulcania's bestiary of mindlessly violent creatures. Any of them, let alone whole stampedes of them, could completely wipe out every person living on this volcanic island."

Each member of Brett's group made eye contact with several of the others, then looked at nothing in particular.

"Oh, no," Merco said, his chipper demeanor deflating. "It happened."

"Yeah," Brett said. "The streets were filled with mangled bodies, limbs, blood ... did you make these creatures? Was this a *Jurassic Park* kind of situation, with you messing with things to find out if you could, without thinking about whether you *should?*"

"Um ... *no*. The dinosaurs, hexenas, and all the rest were here no doubt millennia before I arrived in my boat full of scientific whatsit and my crew of assistants who also happen to be experienced mariners. It just goes to show what you can find on Indeed.com!"

"Merco," Lathrop said with serious disdain in his voice, "you're trying to tell us that there just *happened* to be dinosaurs a couple of hundred feet below the surface of this volcano? And also sea monsters in the vicinity?"

"Oh, yes, the 'sea monsters,' as you call them. I'm afraid that, while the dearly departed first squad of guns for hire"—at that, Brett recalled the shredded uniforms in the wendigo pit—"are responsible for the breach of the tunnel that apparently released these *things* down here unto the poor villagers of Edinburgh of the Seven Seas, it is entirely my fault that there are Ogopogos in the waters surrounding Tristan da Cunha."

Brett knew that name—it was a cryptid sea serpent. "*That* was Ogopogo?"

"You know the animal?"

Stefan said, "Of course we do! *TMI* traveled all the way from Atlanta to British Columbia to get some footage for the show. We saw some things that definitely could have been the Ogopogo—or 'Naitaka,' as it is called in Coast Salish, the indigenous language of that area."

Ravi said, "It also could have been a log. But most likely Ogopogo. We follow the strictest ethical guidelines on our show, and we would never positively identify something as a cryptid unless we were really, really pretty sure about it."

"It destroyed the *Slangkop II* out of Cape Town. It's the supply ship that comes here a couple of times a year?"

"I know the *Slangkop II*. Was Captain Bantu lost?"

"No," Brett said. "He stayed above ground to see if he could find anyone alive and also secure transport for us away from this island, whenever he can arrange for another ship to pick us up. But who knows if any ship less than a battle cruiser will be able to get past the sea monster that *you* let out."

"It was an *accident* that the creature was released from the water-filled cavitation below us. I was testing the ... um, some *equipment* ... when everything went sideways. A large section of the rock separating the Ogopogos' lair from the open ocean was no longer there and the pair of sea serpents were just able to swim out and bring their eight or nine young with them. They will be a terror on the high seas! But only for a time," he finished sadly, "because soon enough mankind will destroy them. Once the outside world hears about the massacre of the Settlement, the island and soon enough my underground workshop will be overrun and every monster killed. Who knows? Maybe the acid-laden plant life will be used as biological weapons. Or would that be *botanical* weapons?" He chuckled at his own wit despite the dire situation.

"Would you please *seize him*," Lathrop sort-of-commanded the soldiers, but all authority had evaporated from his voice. No one moved to seize anyone … or do anything else, in fact, since no one knew what they were dealing with here. They remained in the care anteroom.

Finally, Merco seemed to realize this. "My goodness, what a terrible host I am! You must be reunited with your wife, Mister Russell! All of you, please do come inside and see what I've built here. I'm going to save the world, you know."

"Should we leave the guns or take off our shoes or anything?" Crane asked mulishly, causing Lathrop to almost scream with frustration. "I'm just sayin', it's not like he's gonna be able to sneak away."

"No, by all means, bring your guns! Down here, there's almost always something that might need to get shot. I wish I could shoot all the plants! It makes being on the surface *such* an unpleasant experience." He turned to lead them through the doorway, but stopped and said, "Just to be precise, when I said 'the surface' just now, of course I mean the surface of underground Vulcania. I hope the *surface* surface never has to bear the scourge of those nasty things! I doubt it will, actually, since they seem quite gone off photosynthesis. In any case, onward!"

They followed in single file through the doorway, and as each person passed through, he gasped in awe at the tremendous volume of space they walked into. It was like an airplane hangar; the ceiling of this space must have had the surface immediately above it. In the room, cages lined the wall like a prison, and Brett could see that a fantastic and most likely utterly deadly cryptid was inside each one: there was the jackal-thing, which Merco called a "hexena"; giant insects from their all-too-familiar steel-gray wasp to the megapede to giant ants, beetles, and spiders, which Brett was incredibly grateful they hadn't run into; and even smaller dinosaurs from the size of dogs to that of horses. The cages were set into the wall, so it was impossible to tell how high or deep they were. But every single door had a being in it, gazing wistfully at the dinner just out of reach.

The dinners were people in the room, of which there were (other than Brett, Merco, and the rest of the group) five: Ellie—*Ellie!* It was all Brett could do not to run to her—Natasha, and three men who were busily futzing with some piece of equipment. The room had a great deal of scientific-looking apparatuses and huge computer monitors. But the *pièce de résistance* was the titanic glowing tube across the center of the cavernous space at about twenty feet up: it looked like a horizontally oriented fluorescent light tube at least twenty feet in diameter, shining powerfully enough that it was uncomfortable to look at directly for more than a few seconds.

Brett noticed that everything in the carved-out space—like everywhere else in Merco's domain, the walls, ceiling, and floor were all as smooth as polished marble—was oriented to point at the eerie energy tube in the center. Whatever was going on down there, it was all about that cylinder of light. But what *he* was about down there right then was his ex-wife ... who had apparently left off the "ex" part when talking to Doctor Merco.

That was intriguing.

She sat in an office chair in front of a large table which had, under glass, an equally large map of the world. Various marks had been made over certain spots on the glass over particular places. When Ellie saw Brett enter the room, she quickly stood up and waved happily.

Happily, Brett repeated to himself. Maybe she had told herself she would marry him again if he showed up—if he survived—to rescue her and take her back to civilization. Or she might just have told Merco that they were still married so he'd be more inclined to let him see her. Or something else. It didn't matter, because he was there and she was safe. As nonplussed as he was about Merco's wendigos plucking her away in the first place, he wasn't mad at all at the man now that he saw what good care he had taken of Ellie, who looked none the worse for wear from her travel via giant cryptid.

Brett waved back with a big smile. He still had no idea what was going to happen inside the weird scientist's lair, let alone what they were going to do once they had to go back out into Vulcania, but this sure made the whole disaster feel a lot less disastrous.

Still seated at the table, unmoving, unsmiling, and with no visible reaction to the remainder of her travel mates was the woman they all called Natasha. Maybe she didn't think they'd be able to actually rescue her, or maybe she didn't want whatever rescue they offered, but she looked *unthrilled*, to say the least.

"How rude of me!" Merco cried when he noticed the group looking at Natasha. "Please allow me to introduce my daughter, Nadia."

Nadia! Brett thought with amusement. *I was so close.*

Nadia-not-Natasha didn't wave, move, or blink. This made Merco laugh heartily, and he said, "She's quite the sassy lassie, isn't she? Told the Organization all about what I was doing down here, very naughty of her, indeed. But she didn't count on them forcing her to come down here herself to get me to come back! *Ha, ha!* She hasn't said two words to me since my Ithaqua brought her back, but I know my daughter well enough to know she didn't think any travel would be required for her to earn her millions for selling out her father … and the entire human race, for that matter."

Brett looked at Lathrop. "You knew the whole time why we're going after this guy?"

"I don't feel compelled to tell you anything, Mister Russell," Lathrop said as he avoided meeting the eyes of anyone in the room.

"However, I *choose* to inform you that I was not briefed on the nature of Doctor Merco's superweapon, only told to bring it and him back at any cost."

"You don't *know?*" Merco asked incredulously. "My goodness, do *none* of you know what's going on down here? My dear Nadia didn't tell you how I'm going to save the world? This isn't a 'superweapon,' my friends–it's a *super-savior!* Why don't you all sit at the big table with Nadia and allow me to explain? I guarantee you won't want to stop me once you see what I've done here."

"Actually, Doctor, we haven't the time nor the inclination to listen to whatever crackpot extortion scheme you're planning to use this weapon for. My employer wants you and the weapon delivered to them in Geneva, and that desire has been the subject of considerable investment." Lathrop indicated to Commander Crane to get on with it already. "We will escort you from this hellish island back to Cape Town and then to the Organization Black Ops site at an undisclosed location so you may voluntarily share the offensive strike capability you developed and brought here."

At that, Nadia at the table let out a laugh of irony mixed with bemusement. This threw off Lathrop and Crane–and everyone else present, really–and Merco added to the confusion with a laugh of his own as he said, "My friends, Nadia here is helping me tell you that you can't *bring* this 'capability' anywhere. This island, this *volcano, is* the so-called 'superweapon'!"

While Merco talked, Ellie went for broke and stalked right over to Brett and put her arms around him. They held each other for a moment and looked in each other's eyes. *Yes, indeed*, Brett thought, *we're getting rid of the 'ex.'*

The scientists motioned for them all to have a seat at the large polished conference table at which Nadia sat without further display of human emotion, and Brett and Ellie held hands at the table, freshly enamored even though there was very little chance they or anyone else would be making it back home alive.

Once they were all settled, Merco clicked a few buttons at a console in front of the table, and a large screen came up from the floor. From some automatic control, at the same time as a projector illuminated the screen, the lights in the huge space dimmed enough for Merco to begin his presentation. Brett saw that it had to have been prepared in advance, maybe to show the world the destructive power of his "super-savior" superweapon, maybe just to show Merco's visitors once he knew the expedition was truly on its way to see him.

The first slide that came onto the screen showed a section of the island from a three-quarter angle, a scene obviously constructed from the game *Mineshaft*. It took a moment to see why, but then the graphics choice made total sense. "My plan to save the world from itself began with a completely unrelated discovery. This is what the Organization is after, no doubt, since it could make for an interesting weapon, although to call it a 'superweapon' without the concomitant use of Tristan da Cunha would be a bit of an overstatement." Merco addressed them as if they were a college class: "Now, is anyone here familiar with what physicists call 'zero-point energy'?"

Ravi and Stefan, both dedicated pseudoscience geeks, raised their hands immediately. Brett had also heard the term but had absolutely no idea what it meant, so he kept to himself. Given the *TMI* Team's enthusiasm and Merco's garrulousness, he knew he'd learn exactly what it was in short order.

He was right. Ravi immediately offered, "Big Science won't admit it, but zero-point energy is basically an unlimited, completely free source of infinite power. See, in quantum field theory, the vacuum or 'zero point' state is the quantum state having the lowest possible energy. It doesn't have any mass within it, and Einstein showed that mass equals energy, so it's just the energy of the ground state, which is zero. Hence, 'zero-point energy.'"

"Yes," Merco said, "exactly. And how does it produce this possibly unlimited amount of free power?"

Ravi's expression remained the same, but his eyes went as blank as a corpse's. "I ... don't have the exact numbers in front of me."

Merco laughed. "This is why I love *The Mysterious Investigators!* Yes, I watch your show, don't look so surprised—to me, science is just the shadow cast by mystery."

"I have no idea what that means, but I like it," Stefan said as he videoed the entire thing.

"That should be the motto of your program!" The scientist laughed again. "In any case, I have been able to use the aether equations of Nikola Tesla—'zero point' is really just the modern term for aether theory—to create a zero-point volume out of any region of space. Within the limitations of current technology, of course. This allows me to use the energy of empty space to create another volume of utterly empty space."

The smooth walls and precise cubes cut out of the landscape suddenly made sense to Brett. "You're excavating regular blocks of matter by reducing them to the zero point of the vacuum?"

"Exactly! Well done, sir! This would make a formidable weapon, indeed, and I knew the Organization would fund me well in order to have such an innovation in their power-mad hands. I'm talking about *billions* of dollars here, which the Organization was only too happy to supply as long as they saw consistent progress." He smiled and spread his hands to make a gesture of generosity. "So I gave them consistent progress! As soon as I had the breakthrough and bought the first round of equipment for my laboratory in Switzerland, I was able to create zero-point fields as large as a city block! But I didn't tell the Organization this, of course; I had received only two hundred million dollars or so at that point."

"*Only*," Lathrop repeated in a rancid tone.

"Galling, isn't it?" Merco said with a huge grin. "That money was used to build the equipment, obviously, but also to set up an escrow fund for my Swiss assistants Knisper, Knasper, and Knusper, whom you see here." The assistants, whose names were without a doubt not what Merco said, waved hello with big smiles of their own. "They didn't have to be sworn to secrecy anymore. All they had to do was see this through to the end and the legal team would release their funds. And secrecy has been incredibly important! I made the mistake of telling my daughter, who was how I knew about the existence of the Organization and their unlimited appetite for power and money in the first place, the location of Phase II of my plan. Accessing this subterranean space and carving out my workspace even underneath that is what has taken the lion's share of the four billion dollars the Organization was good enough to provide me with."

"*Five* billion," Lathrop corrected. His tone remained nasty. Brett couldn't say he blamed him, although he *could* say he was enjoying this immensely.

"I know. I just wanted to make you say it, you war-mongering son of a motherless goat." Now Merco pointed out a section of the *Minecraft* Landscape and said, "Once I had the hydrargyrum plates in place, I just cut blocks out of the biomass, *blip blip blip*, and made this entire substructure." Slightly underneath the ground in the cross section on screen, cubes of matter disappeared and were replaced by blackness. "This is how I cut the tunnel down here in the first place. I knew it was going to be a hostile environment, but *hoo boy*, this place is something special. We were able to get through by simply cutting out blocks ahead of us as we moved, but it took a while to charge up the plates every time. Had to evaporate a few dinosaurs and a whole lot of those miserable man-eating plants."

Brett spoke up. "How did you know this was all down here in the first place?"

Merco continued to smile as he addressed Lathrop. "Would you care to handle this question on behalf of your employer? No? All right, then: The Organization has long known there was a kind of 'lost world' down here, written about by Conan Doyle and others through secondhand accounts by Pacific Islanders. Don't ask me how *they* knew in the first place! Perhaps it was open to the rest of the world at some point; I haven't any idea. But the Organization knew, and that information found its way to me, and the information that I had this information found its way back to them via the dastardly Nadia."

Everyone looked at the slim woman, who said nothing.

"Yes, in any case, I knew that the Organization had long been planning to utilize the horrors found beneath the volcano here for paramilitary purposes as they continue to assemble their New World Order." He shook his head at Lathrop, who looked like he was going to explode with pent-up fury. "Alas, I got here first and was able to access the found world by use of my zero-point matter remover. The very inaccessibility of this realm was all that had kept the Organization from harvesting and breeding dinosaurs and giant killer bugs and such to sell to the highest bidder, whether a sovereign government or terrorist group or other unsavory collection of psychopaths."

"I'm not the psychopath here, Merco," Lathrop said. "All I see left from the first commandos who came here is tattered uniforms at the bottom of that monster pit of yours."

For the first time, Merco didn't smile at something Lathrop said. "That is regrettable, although they arrived in this place with every intention of subverting my ultimate plan through violence, so I'm not as worked up about using them as I might otherwise be."

"*Using* them?" Brett asked.

"Yes. I needed to train the wendigos to do what I needed—they are insanely huge and strong, as you saw for yourselves—and feeding them the troop of mercenaries was my only option. But you soldiers needn't worry; everything is finished now, and I have no need of any of the creatures that live down here."

Brett looked again at the cages of strange animals and insects held behind the bars of the cages in the walls of the immense room. "Then why are they here?"

"Well, I *am* a scientist! We have a full workup on every one of the cryptids that I and my team have encountered in this underground biome. I have all the reports on my Google Drive. I can share them with you if I get your email address when all of this is done."

Ravi, Stefan, and Ellie practically drooled at the thought of all that material for the next ten years of *TMI* episodes. It was probably all they could do not to blurt out their emails right then and there.

"So, if the superweapon—or super-savior—isn't the cool zero-point block vaporizer, then what is it?" Brett asked, and he could see that everyone in his group had the exact same question.

"The five billion dollar question, eh?" Merco said with relish as he teased the miserable Lathrop. "You may find it hard to believe, but I have devised a way to give humankind an extra two to three years of survival, two to three years during which global warming will be *put on hold* and the countries of the world will be given this time to come to some workable strategy to stop climate change. It's increasing exponentially, as I'm sure you know, but my idea is about to not only flatten the rate of growth flat or even make it arithmetical—it will stop the growth in its tracks for, as I say, long enough for the nations of Earth to overcome their folly and save the human race from extinction."

Brett blinked and looked at Ellie, who also seemed completely taken aback by the scientist's assertion. "That, um, sounds like a tall order."

"Doesn't it? But it's all based on much more solid science than zero-point energy, and I was able to make *that* work!" He advanced the presentation slide to one showing the island with its volcano as it would appear from a ship a few miles offshore. The diagram showed the massive lava tube stretching up from the superheated magma chamber directly to the top of the volcano. There were also secondary vents in addition to that epically huge main vent. "This volcano last erupted in 1961, but before that had never gone off in modern times. This eruption was only through the secondary vents you see here; the main vent has been building in pressure since the advent of humanity. There isn't much chance of a major eruption for decades, if not centuries, if not millennia, due to this thick blockage of rock below the surface of the island—just east of us down here, in fact. This illuminated tube points straight at it."

In a flash, it dawned on Brett where this was going … or at least most of it. "You're going to disintegrate the rock so that the magma can flow and the volcano will erupt."

"It's not *disintegration* so much as complete removal, but yes. With the amount of pent-up energy contained within the magma chamber, tens of thousands of years' worth, it will be an explosion to rival that of Krakatoa. And that, my friends, is the whole point of this entire escapade: when Krakatoa blew, it sounded like a cannon being fired to people in England, *seven thousand miles away*. It threw up so much ash into the atmosphere that the average temperature everywhere on the planet increased by three degrees Fahrenheit. There were record snowfalls around the world, and things didn't heat back up to normal for two to three years." Merco smiled as he saw it click with each person there (except Crane, who obviously didn't know what Krakatoa was). "I'm talking about Krakatoa because it's the most famous giant volcanic explosion, but in 1815, the Indonesian volcano Mount Tambora cooled the world even more, completely vaporizing its home island. So powerful was this eruption that the next year, 1816, is known as 'the year without a summer.' My Tristan da Cunha eruption will rival even Tambora. If this intermission in warming doesn't provide a chance for the people at the top to make a change, then nothing will. It's the least I can do as a member of the human race."

"And all the nations of the world will just cut emissions because of this? Will they even think of this as an opportunity to do that?"

"I have little faith in nation-states and even less in NGOs like the Organization to figure out any positive in the world for themselves. No, I have an automated transmission that will be sent out starting an hour before the volcano erupts: it will announce to every news outlet, big or small, why this is being done and the unique, unprecedented opportunity this represents. It'll also go out to the public directly via the Web," Merco said. "I will ask my assistants to leave the island so they are not killed. Unfortunately, Vulcania and everything living on, under, or near it will be destroyed along with the island itself. That's why I was so careful to collect and preserve the data from these strange animals and plants.

"I was concerned," Merco continued, "about how I might be able to convince the residents of Edinburgh of the Seven Seas to leave their homes, but it seems that the idiot mercenaries removing the gate to the surface has allowed our cryptid predators to decide those unfortunate people's fates. I, of course, will die in the explosion, but I'd be a dead man anyway once the volcano blows its top. I would be hunted by every country in the world *and* the Organization. It's better to go down with the ship, I think."

"This is preposterous," Lathrop said, and took to his feet. "You aren't blowing up this island for some idiot scheme to save the world. Do you have any idea how much the Organization has invested in the current energy paradigm? I ask this rhetorically, because you wouldn't believe it if I told you. It makes an amount almost equal to that initial investment *every single year*. They're not going to let you ruin that—*I* won't let you ruin it. Crane, you and your man take this bastard into custody after he tells you where the plans are for his zero-point energy apparatus."

"I have a large speedboat on the other side of the island, Mister …"

"Lathrop."

"Splendid. Greetings, Mister Lathrop. As I say, I have a means to get away from the island in a hurry. Captain Bantu won't have to wait a month for a ship to take you back to Cape Town—I designed a special fuel cell that will take that speedboat all the way for my assistants to escape, but there would be room for the rest of you as well. It might be a little cramped, but well worth it to save your lives, hm?"

"I've been living inside of a wasp shell," Ravi said. "I don't know about anyone else, but at this point I can take a close boat ride."

"Crane, do I have to do this myself? This is what you're getting paid for! *Now! Seize him!*"

Crane and Flattop obeyed this time: they stood, pulled out their sidearms, and moved toward the scientist. He saw this and leaned down to the computer on the table next to where he was standing. He clicked a couple of times with the mouse, then, oddly, turned his head to the side while he typed madly and randomly on the keyboard. Then he looked back, punched a series of keys and clicked twice with the mouse, then straightened. "Do with me as you will, gentlemen. But only I know where the keys to the speedy Organization-funded watercraft are located."

"Don't worry," Lathrop said with a renewed sneer of confidence, "we'll get that information out of you in due time, Doctor."

"Time." Merco laughed. "Time is not on your side, Mister Lathrop. I just activated the timer for this gargantuan zero-point machine. It's set for three hours, just enough time to get off this island and sail far enough away not to be completely erased from the face of the Earth along with Tristan da Cunha."

Lathrop turned pale and said, "You're bluffing."

"Bluffing? I don't really see what the advantage would be to misrepresenting the situation here, but as you can see behind me, my assistants are already gathering their things to move out." And Brett could see that this was true. He highly doubted Merco was bluffing, and he also highly doubted anyone could get back through Vulcania and off the island in the time allotted by the zero-point machine's countdown. They were all as good as dead … unless Merco was bluffing. Which, again, Brett really didn't think he was.

Like Crane, Flattop hadn't moved an inch since Merco made it clear only be could stop the island from blowing up now that it was on its way. He now asked, "Even if we're far enough away not to get wiped out by the explosion itself, won't, like, a giant tsunami come and wipe us out anyway?"

"Excellent question!" Doctor Merco cried with glee. (Brett suspected he had been a teacher at some point in the way to his PhD.) "Actually, miles away from the epicenter of the eruptive earthquake, the sea will rise a few meters, but the wavelength of a tsunami is so long that nobody on the boat will probably even notice. Tidal waves in the movies are these sharp peaks, but no tsunami is like that in real life."

Sure, Brett thought, *because the rest of this place is SO like real life*.

"Anyway, you'd all better get going, then," Merco said, literally making the motion to shoo them along. Crane and Flattop, who each held in their hands a locked-and-loaded Kalashnikov purchased from a Ukrainian dealer in illegal arms, just nodded and turned to go before Lathrop completely lost his cool.

"*Goddamned idiots!*" he screamed, then stepped up and grabbed Flattop's AK-47 from his hands. He pointed it at Doctor Merco and commanded in a voice quavering with anger and frustration, "Turn that off *right now* and get the goddamned plans and notes for the zero-point weapon. Then get your ass out that door." He motioned at the entrance to the enormous space from where they had come.

"Your fancy talkin' seems to have taken a coffee break," Brett said with a mocking smile.

Lathrop let loose a string of expletives that no one would have called "fancy."

"You kiss your money with that mouth?"

The barrel of the AK-47 swung to point at Brett. "You know this is loaded, right? I don't actually have any further need of you, Mister Russell. It would be nothing to me to pull this trigger and kill you *and* your ex-wife."

"Aw," the old romantic Merco moaned.

"It's okay," Brett said. "I think we might be giving things another try."

"Huzzah!"

"*Shut the hell up, all of you!*" Lathrop shrieked, looking ready to pull the trigger on all three of them.

"But, seriously, he's not going to shoot me or Ellie."

The Organization man's eye twitched and he lifted the sight of the rifle to his eye. "And why's that?"

"Because you owe me payment. If you kill me, everyone will know you didn't pay up, and I'm thinking they'll kill you because then they would know you don't plan to pay them, either. Obviously, you're not going to kill the doctor, the man you came so far for." He pointed a thumb at Ellie. "And if you kill her, they'll probably just kill you on principle."

Lathrop looked around: while no one actually nodded or made any sound of agreement, nobody shook their head or made any sound of *dis*agreement, either. "Fine. Everybody lives. But I will shoot Doctor Merco in the kneecap if he doesn't get those plans and lead us to safety. He may plan to die in three hours, but he'll sincerely wish to be dead the instant after I shoot him there, literally the most painful spot on the human body in which to be injured." He was the one smiling now. "And I'm going to keep him alive for weeks!"

"You don't understand," Merco said, completely calmly as if he hadn't just been threatened with torture unto death. He also hadn't moved to collect whatever plans he had for the zero-point device ... or to do anything else, for that matter. "Everyone in this room can die. Every animal known or unknown to man on this island can die. This entire island can disappear. None of it matters in the face of ending climate change and saving the rest of humanity."

Lathrop laughed icily. "Oh, come now! You can't possibly be that Pollyannaish—the politicians are going to do *nothing*. Or, rather, I envision them using this three-year respite from global warming to ramp up production at every factory that emits CO_2 into the air, to take all mileage restrictions off automobiles, and on and on! Your mission is doomed to failure. It's not worth losing your life over, you old fool."

"Like the Organization isn't going to kill him anyway," Brett said. Although he knew for an iron-clad fact that Lathrop was right—it just wasn't human nature to make that kind of commitment to save the world—he stood and walked over to one of the extra weapons bags. Still under gunpoint by a gradually disbelieving Lathrop, he pulled out one of the other AK-47s. He switched off the safety and pointed it back at Lathrop, who looked like he literally thought he was dreaming. "So cut the crap. Let's all just try to get out of here in one piece while we still can, huh? Doctor Merco, I'm sorry, man—but you have to come with us off the island. They're paying me only if you get back to Cape Town, and I need to get paid. It's not money, if that helps." *Why would that help?* Brett thought. *Whatever. Shut up. You don't have to enjoy it.*

For the first time, Merco looked distressed. *Very* distressed. "B-But … w-why aren't you shooting this malefactor?" he said to Brett while backing up into another computer station, this one with a large red plunger button on it. "You have the weapon! Why don't you just kill him?"

Brett knew it was desperation that drove Merco's words, but he couldn't help himself at this latest suggestion for him to "just" kill someone. "For one, because then I wouldn't get paid," he said, "and for another, because I'm not willing to *be a murderer*."

Merco placed the palm of his hand just above the red button on the desk. "No? Well, to save the world, I *am*," he uttered in a suddenly distant voice. "I'm so very sorry, everyone." Then, before Brett or any of the suddenly panicked and screaming laboratory assistants could stop him, he brought his palm down on the button.

A klaxon sounded, loud enough to make everyone double in pain with their hands over their ears. Spinning red emergency lights threw the vast cavern's walls and ceiling into relief, the only space not flickering with their demonic color being the brilliantly white tube of illumination belonging to the zero-point device. But the most alarming, the most *horrifying* result of Merco mashing whatever that big button could have been was the metal doors to every one of the imprisoned cryptids' cages.

The monsters had been loosed.

"There is a direct tunnel to the marina through that door!" Merco shouted to them at the top of his lungs. "Go! Go *now!*"

"You're coming with us!" Lathrop shouted, still pointing the Kalashnikov at him. "I'll shoot, goddamnit!"

"I don't doubt it!" Merco said with a huge smile—

—and threw himself into the mouth of a hexena that was running at them. The six-legged jackal-thing didn't stop running even as he crushed Merco's torso between its teeth and shook him until his neck was broken and he hung there like a duck in the jaws of a hunting dog.

"*Oh, my God!*" Ellie yelled, which were Brett's sentiments exactly.

The room had exploded into human screams and animal roars, plus the buzz of the wasp that had taken flight. It zipped all the way to the distant ceiling, then swung like a stunt pilot and dived within five feet of the floor, whereupon it hurled its stinger forward and punched it right through Flattop the commando, exploding his guts out the front of his body and covering Stefan, the camera lens, and Ravi with gore.

"Tell me you got that," Ravi said, and Stefan nodded with incredible happiness.

You two are insane, Brett thought, but had to put a pin in that while he pushed Ellie out of the way of *what the hell is that a freaking land shark* and unloaded into it with the submachine gun. The 7.62mm rounds tore nicely through its rough hide and fin-feet, not only stopping it in its headlong rush but actually shoving it back as it tore the abominable cryptid into chunks.

"Thanks," Ellie said in the voice of shock.

"Mention it," Brett said, then yelled to the three lab assistants who were almost to the door out to the marina but were also between Brett and the two ravening velociraptors coming up from behind them, "*Nerds! Get down!*"

They followed his instructions and hit the deck; the instant they were out of his line of fire, he unloaded into those fierce-but-come-on-so-clichéd dinosaurs and dropped them like sacks of corn. The lab assistants didn't have to be told to make a run for it—they were out the door before the ringing faded in Brett's ears.

Now for the rest of them. Ravi and Stefan (whose camera lens was now wiped off) stood back to back, which was a good defensive move if you didn't then completely freeze in place, like the two documentarians now had. A snake so massive it made the green anaconda look like a garden hose opened, a snake that was eight feet in diameter, slithered forward and opened its mouth to sweep them inside.

But something little and gray flew into its mouth, causing the snake to close it instinctively. Then a very loud but muffled *bang* and the head burst open, its earthball-sized eyes slamming into computer monitors twenty feet away.

Brett wiped the snake entrails out of his eyes and looked in the direction the grenade had come from: Ellie stood there, ten feet to his left, and gave him a thumbs-up. "You are *bringin' it!*" he yelled to her.

"*Ain't I, though?*" she yelled back.

Brett grabbed Ravi and Stefan by the collars and shoved them toward the exit. "Get out of here!" When they didn't immediately run, he shouted, "What the hell are you doing? *Go!*"

"But … the footage," Stefan said.

Brett thought his head was going to explode, but before he could scream at them, a swamp monster howled and ran for them, dragging slime behind it. The two shrieked like girls and got themselves through the door before anything else could get them. It tried to follow them out, but a line shot through the air and the grappling hook sank into the monster's body and wrapped around one of its root vines. It was stuck.

On the other end of the grappling hook was Crane. He tied the line off around a railing and said with a laugh, "I'm a damn good soldier, if I may say so myself," and a Chupacabra jumped him from behind and ate his head.

Brett dispatched it with three shots and gave the headless body of Commander Crane a nod of respect: he really was a pretty good soldier.

It was time to get himself and Ellie and Lathrop out of there. And Natasha/Nadia. *In fact, where is ...*

He scanned the area for the table where she had been sitting. He found it, and at the same time found Nadia the Organization Connection. Her body was now on top of the table. It had been split into two messy halves, no doubt by a disagreement between the two heads of the Maltese lizard-tiger now feeding on her.

Okay, so himself and Ellie and Lathrop. Ellie was next to him now, and he yelled, "Grab a gun bag and get out of here! I'll be right behind you!"

She looked at him a little askance—she knew he damn well couldn't promise that—but nodded, ran, shot a charging Yeti right in the face, and ran some more until she passed out of sight into the escape tunnel.

Now there was just Lathrop, who cowered under the big table on top of which the Maltese cryptid was chewing with both mouths on the corpse of Doctor Merco's daughter. It galled him to do so, but he shot and fought his way over to Lathrop, crouching down to pull him out of there and save his rotten neck so he could pay Brett what he was owed. It wasn't Brett's fault that the scientist killed himself; Brett's job was to head the expedition and, if they found him, make sure Merco was kept alive while they worked their way out of this underground world. Lathrop was going to give him the name of whoever was responsible for the murder of his family.

"Come on, man, this place is going to blow," Brett said, putting out his hand to help Lathrop out from under the table.

"I'm not going anywhere, Mister Russell. I am as good as dead once the Organization learns that I failed. I might as well die less excruciatingly by staying here."

"Yeah, no problem. Just tell me how to get the information you have locked away in Cape Town." A realization hit him, something he had feared all along but had to ignore: "There *is* no information, is there?"

"Yes, there is, and it is safe in South Africa. Unfortunately, the secure premises' operator will open the box only with me present. I do apologize, Mister Russell, but I'm afraid—" *WHOCK!* Brett popped him in the face with the butt of his AK-47, knocking him unconscious. He dragged Lathrop out and lifted him onto his shoulders in a fireman's carry. All that was between himself and the exit to the boat now was a needle-toothed crawling merman, a dinosaur-cryptid that looked like a cross between a *Stegosaurus* and a *Velociraptor*, a cobra-like six-foot Tsuchinoko, a Zululand native walking poisonous tree called the Umdhlebi, a Wampus cat, a hippogriff with blood smeared all over its beak, and ten-foot walking bugs, twelve-foot flying bugs, and a bug so tall that its bloated body was lost in the shadows near the ceiling. How it had fit out of one of the cage doors to get into the large space was too weird to think about.

He wished he had one of the hollowed-out wasp carcasses to conceal and protect himself as he made a run for the exit, but all he had was the guns to fend them off. But he and Lathrop were the only fresh meat still in the room, and the various creatures seemed to realize this one by one.

He shot three different creatures, which made most every one of the others jerk a little with surprise, but it didn't keep them back. And the third bullet didn't startle them as much as the second, which didn't as much as the first. He didn't have enough bullets for them all.

They were about to close it, and Brett wouldn't be able to keep them away if he had unlimited bullets once they got close enough. And he couldn't set off either kind of grenade, concussion or shrapnel, because it would go off too close to himself if the things wouldn't let him slip by.

Animals, cryptids, dinosaurs, and bugs, and carrying an asshole on my shoulders. This is how I'm going out. It was his usual ironic patter to himself, but he heard *bug* as if someone else were saying it in his ear. *Bug, bug, bug ... spray?* There were four big canisters of the bug repellent in the weapons bags … and there were multi-purpose cigarette lighters. He hadn't done this since he was in middle school, but he'd maybe pulling the ultimate MacGyver trick would do what bullets and grenades no longer could in this situation. *You're not afraid of bullets*, he thought, *but I bet you're afraid of fire.*

Balancing the dead weight of the Organization man, he slowly went to his knees to get at the nearest equipment duffle. A couple of seconds felt like an eternity, but it took him just a couple of seconds to grab the thick can of insect repellent, grab a lighter, stand, press the spray trigger, and flick the Bic. A thick tongue of flame leapt forth, and every monster without exception leapt back in terror.

He kept the bug spray flowing out of the can and kept the lighter flame right in front of it and he walked—quickly, but there was no way to run with a man over his shoulders while he kept the makeshift flamethrower going—right through the retreating cryptid horror show and out the tunnel. He dropped the spray can and the lighter, then, despite the load on his shoulders, ran like hell.

~~~

One year later, Brett Russell sat with his wife, Ellie, in a car at Christchurch Airport on the South Island of New Zealand. They were headed to New York City for their first time back in the United States since the Great Cooling started. The global weather effect began with the supervolcanic explosion of Tristan da Cunha less than three hours after Captain Bantu got them off and away from the doomed island. Since then, *The Mysterious Investigators* relocated to New Zealand, which invited them after *TMI* broadcast some very tourism-board-friendly discoveries regarding hobbits and other Tolkien cryptids alleged to exist in the country's mountains. That show was seen by millions, as were most episodes since *TMI* shared the footage from Tristan da Cunha.

Brett stayed in New Zealand because Ellie was going to be there. It was always possible that the Organization might have spotted him there and sent a hitman or whatever they did to silence anyone they didn't want alive, but it never happened. They might have assumed he died in the massive event, if they ever even knew that Lathrop had hired Brett, Ellie, and the rest. The Organization was sure to have seen the footage from Vulcania and known that the crew was there, but they never made the connection. Part of that might have been that Stefan meticulously edited the video so that Brett was never seen or heard or referred to at any time. Nice work, that.

Or maybe they figured that when, six months after Tristan da Cunha, an overeager contract killer blew Lathrop's brains out before he could be questioned (resulting in a second contract killer killing the first one), they were forced to assume Brett Russell really was dead and would never bother them again.

If so, they figured wrong. He was alive, and he was very much going to bother them.

"So, this is it," Ellie said. "New York. Where ... what's his name again? I keep shutting it out of my brain."

He said the name.

"God, that's an awful name."

"Awful guy."

She nodded, a tear just forming in the corner of one eye. "Just ... God, be careful. If you *can* be careful doing this."

"I'm not afraid of the Organization anymore."

"I know *that*," she said. "But if the police catch you before you can get back home ... you'll never get back home."

"They won't. I've got this. It's time for that old life to be settled so our new one can start."

She nodded again, and they held each other for a minute before a taxi honked behind them and reminded them this was not a designated stopping zone. They kissed, then he got his bag and got out, waving to her as she pulled away.

Then, like a blessing over the holy duty, he was traveling to perform, the news crawl over the entrance to the airport read:

ALL NATIONS SIGN ON TO 'ONE TIME ONLY OPPORTUNITY' CLIMATE CHANGE DEAL

He'd never been so glad to be wrong in his life. He took it in with a smile for a moment, then continued into the airport.

SEVEREDPRESS

facebook.com/severedpress
twitter.com/severedpress

CHECK OUT OTHER GREAT DINOSAUR THRILLERS

JURASSIC ISLAND
by Viktor Zarkov

Guided by satellite photos and modern technology a ragtag group of survivalists and scientists travel to an uncharted island in the remote South Indian Ocean. Things go to hell in a hurry once the team reaches the island and the massive megalodon that attacked their boats is only the beginning of their desperate fight for survival.

Nothing could have prepared billionaire explorer Joseph Thornton and washed up archaeologist Christopher "Colt" McKinnon for the terrifying prehistoric creatures that wait for them on JURASSIC ISLAND!

K-REX
by L.Z. Hunter

Deep within the Congo jungle, Circuitz Mining employs mercenaries as security for its Coltan mining site. Armed with assault rifles and decades of experience, nothing should go wrong. However, the dangers within the jungle stretch beyond venomous snakes and poisonous spiders. There is more to fear than guerrillas and vicious animals. Undetected, something lurks under the expansive treetop canopy...

Something ancient.

Something dangerous.

Kasai Rex!

SEVEREDPRESS

facebook.com/severedpress
twitter.com/severedpress

CHECK OUT OTHER GREAT DINOSAUR THRILLERS

WRITTEN IN STONE
by David Rhodes

Charles Dawson is trapped 100 million years in the past. Trying to survive from day to day in a world of dinosaurs he devises a plan to change his fate. As he begins to write messages in the soft mud of a nearby stream, he can only hope they will be found by someone who can stop his time travel. Professor Ron Fontana and Professor Ray Taggit, scientists with opposing views, each discover the fossilized messages. While attempting to save Charles, Professor Fontana, his daughter Lauren and their friend Danny are forced to join Taggit and his group of mercenaries. Taggit does not intend to rescue Charles Dawson, but to force Dawson to travel back in time to gather samples for Taggit's fame and fortune. As the two groups jump through time they find they must work together to make it back alive as this fast-paced thriller climaxes at the very moment the age of dinosaurs is ending.

HARD TIME
by Alex Laybourne

Rookie officer Peter Malone and his heavily armed team are sent on a deadly mission to extract a dangerous criminal from a classified prison world. A Kruger Correctional facility where only the hardest, most vicious criminals are sent to fend for themselves, never to return.

But when the team come face to face with ancient beasts from a lost world, their mission is changed. The new objective: Survive.

SEVEREDPRESS

facebook.com/severedpress
twitter.com/severedpress

CHECK OUT OTHER GREAT DINOSAUR THRILLERS

SPINOSAURUS
by Hugo Navikov

Brett Russell is a hunter of the rarest game. His targets are cryptids, animals denied by science. But they are well known by those living on the edges of civilization, where monsters attack and devour their animals and children and lay ruin to their shantytowns.

When a shadowy organization sends Brett to the Congo in search of the legendary dinosaur cryptid Kasai Rex, he will face much more than a terrifying monster from the past. Spinosaurus is a dinosaur thriller packed with intrigue, action and giant prehistoric predators.

LAND OF DEATH
by Eric S Brown & Alex Laybourne

A group of American soldiers, fleeing an organized attack on their base camp in the Middle East, encounter a storm unlike anything they've seen before. When the storm subsides, they wake up to find themselves no longer in the desert and perhaps not even on Earth. The jungle they've been deposited in is a place ruled by prehistoric creatures long extinct. Each day is a struggle to survive as their ammo begins to run low and virtually everything they encounter, in this land they've been hurled into, is a deadly threat.

Printed in Poland
by Amazon Fulfillment
Poland Sp. z o.o., Wrocław